ADVENTUROUS CHILDREN OF THE DONNER PARTY

by

HOLLY WILSON BENNETT

To my own adventurous grandchildren,
Andrew, Adrian and Paige Bennett.

Table of Contents

Preface

A Lumber Camp - Donner Lake, California, 1891

Kneeling on the uneven, unyielding ground, Edward leaned to the right, then to the left, and finally backwards, hands on his hips, to ease his aching back. Rising to his feet stiffly, he gazed at his handiwork. He had been hand-mining this rocky, granite area for hours. Surely, there had been flashes of quartz in the stone walls giving him momentary flushes of joy only to be hewn apart into worthless rubble with the quick work on his pickaxe. These stone walls that shaped the rugged hills in the Sierra Mountains were not giving forth their secrets or their treasure. He glanced up the steep incline that reached to the jagged summit of, what was soon to be known as, Donner Pass. Sighing, lifting off his hat, and wiping his damp forehead with his red bandana, he resumed his chip, chip, chip- -the slow process of hand mining. Goodness, he had been swinging his pick away at for what seemed ages. Oh, the process was slow. The wretched rock walls chipped into tiny fragments revealing little more rock. Being a quartz miner meant long, hot days of dusty, hard work. Ah, but when you found the dense quartz lined with veins of gold, oh, how the tiredness melted away. Then you worked feverishly, never tiring as the deeper you penetrated, the more flecks and lines of gold you discovered.

Edward Reynolds was one of many miners who had come down through the Truckee to seek his fortune in California. There was gold, silver, and quartz in the mountains. The treasures were there waiting for the industrious miner to hack it out. Edward was one of thousands who had decided this was how he would make his fortune. He mined to find the quartz and the gold that could be found in the quartz.

By now, he had created a three by three feet   depression and figured from the bright disc of light traveling halfway across the sky that it had to be chow time. He dropped his axe into the hole and crack, it hit something hard. What was that? He wondered. It sounded almost metallic. What could it be? All his other tools were up on a ledge. Grabbing his pick, he leaned down into the small pit and scooped at the ground. Something was there. He unearthed a cloth-wrapped bundle and beheld a wondrous treasure: gold! No, it wasn't gold nuggets. Nor what he held in his hand was quartz with globs of gold. Instead, he held several gold and silver coins. Where had they come from?

Examining each of the heavy coins, he noticed that all bore small, raised numbers indicating a date, but none were dated later than 1845. *Calculating the years, they must be over forty-six years old, he thought.* He sat back on his weathered, dusty boots and remembered that not many years ago a group of immigrants had traveled west on a long, treacherous journey from Illinois to California. It had been in 1846.

Chapter One

Preparing to Go – Springfield, Illinois, 1846

"Patty, call your sister inside to get ready for dinner. I'm expecting your father to come home early," Mrs. Reed called to her youngest daughter who was sitting under an apple tree shelling peas for dinner.

"Yes, Mother." Patty picked up the crockery bowl of shelled peas and the wooden bowl holding pea casings. She set the crockery bowl carefully on the porch steps and headed toward the barn carrying the wooden bowl of pea green shells for the horses. Hearing their nickers when she opened the barn door, she smiled to herself. She diplomatically divided the greens in small portions, opened her hands wide, and held them out to the horses. Their velvet snuffles nuzzled against her palms.

"Patty!" her mother called again.

"Oh, yes." Patty's face slid into a grimace at her mother's rebuke, and she ran out the barn door and all the way to the top of the ridge which gave her a view of the barn, the corral, and their house. Although it was winter, it was a mild day. The trees dressed in January's few dismal leaves with a few old birds' nests dotted on their skeletal network of bare, gray limbs contrasted with the waning light of day. Down below, she saw her stepsister, Virginia, riding her pony. Patty waved, but Virginia did not see her. Patty cupped her hands around her mouth and shouted, "Virginia! Virginia! Time for chores!" Her breath exploded out from her cupped hands. In the distance she could see the short breath snorts spurting from the muzzle of Virginia's pony. Virginia looked up, smiled, waved, and clucked Billy to a trot.

Patty danced with excitement. When Virginia crested the hill, she said, "I think this is the night. We'll take the family vote and..."

"Look," Virginia shouted pointing at two men on horseback, one riding a huge grey and the other a bay in the distance.

"It's father and Milt! Oh, do you think he said yes?" Patty turned to Virginia, but her sister had already taken off at a gallop to join her father and their handyman.

"Virgggiiinia," Patty wailed, running after her. She caught up to the threesome as Virginia flung herself off the pony and into the outstretched arms of her father who had already dismounted.

Milford Elliott put out his arm as Patty stumbled and literally ran into them. "Hold on there, Miss Mattie. Goodness, you'd think we were long-lost family!" He grinned down at her as she fixed her apron over her dress.

Putting her hands on her hips, she corrected him indignantly, "Patty, that's Patty." Her real name was Martha Jane, but she preferred Patty, would suffer with Mattie, but never with Martha!

Milt laughed.

"Are you here for the family vote?" asked Virginia, turning from her father to Milt. Although the family meeting was that evening, they had been talking for several months about moving out West. The girls were anxious to pack up their household and join the wagon trains heading to the Western Frontier.

"Maybe," Milt replied grinning.

Margaret Reed came to the door and, wiping her hands, said, "There won't be a family vote until the horses are brushed, fed, and watered." Pointing to the bowl of peas on the steps, she continued, "Those don't look like they are ready for dinner, do they now?" She smiled at her daughter, Patty, softening her words. "Get busy, girls."

"Yes'm," they both chorused. Patty picked up the bowl and carried the shelled peas into the kitchen giving them to the cook, Eliza. Eliza shook her head as she walked back into the kitchen. *Children*, she thought to herself.

Virginia collected all three horses' sets of reins and set off to the barn.

"Eliza, Father, and Milt are here!" Patty informed her.

Mrs. Reed came to the door and said, "I think everyone knows they are here." She smiled, waved, and went back into the kitchen again. Taking a large breath in through her nose, Eliza took pies from the oven. The fragrant aroma of a freshly baked blackberry pies wafted through the kitchen.

"Those smell heavenly, Eliza."

"They sure do and I can't wait for a slice," agreed Patty.

"There will be plenty for supper and thank you for the peas. I was thinking I'd have to ask Jimmy to go pick some more for the supper table," she chided Patty gently.

"Sorry Eliza, did you hear Pa and Milt are here?"

"Yes, I did hear you call that out. One would have to be deaf not to know that. Now wash up and how about helping Jimmy set the table?" Patty nodded and left.

Virginia returned from her chores with the horses and went to wash up as well.

The family: father, mother, grandmother, Patty, Virginia, Tommy, and Jimmy sat at the table with Milt. Little Jim was five years old and Tommy was three. Their grandmother, Mrs. Sarah Keyes, was quite elderly, but she had sharp eyes and ears and she was insistent that she would follow her daughter Margaret to California.

While Mr. Reed carved the roast, large bowls of creamy mashed potatoes, bright green peas, and fluffy biscuits with fresh peach preserves were passed around the table. Milk from the morning milking and a small plate with freshly churned butter were also passed. Patty helped her brothers, who sat on both sides to her. She made sure they had enough meat, potatoes, and vegetables. She found if she fussed over them, she could keep her excitement at bay. She looked around the table and caught her father's eye.

The discussion at dinner was lively. Her father looked around the table at his family, caught Patty looking at him, and smiled broadly at her. Then he looked back at everyone else gathered at the table. Their excitement was palpable and he was pleased that everyone was considering his proposal to move to the California Territory. His stepdaughter, Virginia Blackenstoe Reed, was seated at his right chattering away to Patty about riding her pony behind the wagon train. She looked up.

"I can ride and save room in the wagon," Virginia said to Milt.

James Reed marveled at Virginia's flair for adventure. She was his wife's daughter by a previous marriage, but he could not have loved her more if she were his own daughter.

Eight-year-old Patty was the more practical of the two sisters and had been elated when her father had asked Milt to consider moving to the Territory with them.

"Can I ride sometimes too?" Jimmy asked.

Milt nodded his head at Jimmy from across the table. Milt sat next to Margaret's mother. Although quite old, she had a gentle way with her grandchildren and he knew she would be a calming force on the long trip out west. He smiled fondly at her. "It will be an adventure," she said, returning his smile.

Several wagon trains had already made their way across the prairies and all the way to the Western Frontier the year before. It was increasingly common for people to move all of their household possessions on wagons clear out to the Pacific Coast. Everyone seemed to be catching the "Go West" fever. The Reed family was no different.

"They say the winters are mild and the vegetation stays lush all year long," Mr. Reed recounted what he had heard from different gatherings of local businessmen. Many of the pioneers who had already "gone west" were writing letters to their friends and families back home about the new frontier. "They pick berries all winter," Mr. Reed continued. "And the apples, oranges, and other fruits and berries are there for the picking. Winter or spring, food is plentiful. Can you imagine, not having to shovel snow, or having weather warm enough to grow crops all year long?" He shook his head in wonderment.

"They say the weather around Sutter's Fort is so wonderful that everything grows. *And*," he emphasized as he saw his wife loo around their beautiful dining room and salon, "we can take our furniture, our trunks, and wardrobes. We will take everything we have. Nothing gets left behind."

Mrs. Reed smiled at him. She had been afraid she would have to leave many of her lovely things. However, she had heard of families taking everything and setting up their new homes in the rugged wilderness with all the lovely things they had before.

"I hear that the roadway to the California Territories is quite wide and easily passable," Milt said. "They say over 500 wagons passed that way last year."

"That's right, Milt. More and more families are tiring of these long, cold winters and want larger farms to till. They're packing up and going west. Also, don't forget Sutter's Fort is not far away from where we plan to settle. It will be as simple as rigging up the horses."

"What is a real fort like?" asked Virginia.

"They're not huge cities, but they're said to be as busy as Springfield here. And they're getting busier and livelier all the time because of all of the people moving to the Oregon or California Territory," Mr. Reed added.

Patty and Virginia looked wide-eyed at their father then at each other. Oh, what fun going out west was going to be! For months now they'd heard their father's stories about the beautiful land and the easy trip out there.

Patty looked at her mother. Mrs. Reed smiled and looked across the table at her own mother. Margaret worried about how the journey would be for her mother, who was now 70-years-old. Mrs. Keyes' health was failing, but for Margaret to take the trip without her be¬loved mother was out of the question. She was afraid that the rigors of many months on a hot, dusty trail would take its toll.

Patty noticed the concern on her mother's face. She herself was worried for her grandmother too, but she knew there was no way they would leave without her. Patty had thought about offering to stay in Springfield if her grandmother didn't feel up for making the long trip. But her grandmother was feisty and would not allow others to make concessions for her. She had grown up in the wilderness. She had grown up fearing bears, wolves, and Indians; a trip across the country in a wagon did not sound so impossible to her. She would not be left behind.

Mrs. Keyes looked into the concerned eyes around her and said, "I'd love to see California." She knew her children wanted to make this trip. "I will make the trip just fine. And I will be able to see my other son again."

Seeing the worry on his wife's and his mother-in-law's faces, Mr. Reed boomed, "You shall indeed see those cities, Grandmother Keyes. As soon as we are settled in California, we shall all take a trip to visit them."

"Can I go to California too, Pa?" asked Little Jim who had been quietly listening to the conversation thinking of Indians. Along with the stories of land as far as you could see and the need for all labor skills to help build up the new territories, they had also heard that some of the Indians attacked the wagon trains and then others helped the pioneers.

"Yes, you too! Milt will drive all of us there."

"Me too?" interrupted Tommy. "I want to go."

"Of course, you too," said Mrs. Reed gently. "I would never leave without you."

"Is it safe?" wondered Jimmy, still thinking about the Indians.

"Of course it will be safe," Milt assured him. "Your Pa and I will be there. And remember, many others have already gone before us and have set up homesteads and businesses."

"It will be safe because Cash will be there to protect us," Tommy declared confidently. He knew his dog, Cash, was the bravest of dogs and would protect all of them from Indians and bears. "Cash will keep the bears and the Indians away," he said with certainty.

The adults laughed and sat back enjoying their coffee.

"Don't forget about all of the things you will see. New towns and cities, and there is a port not far from the fort, New Helvitia, I think, so goods from across the sea will be arriving every few days. Plus, they will need to ship out all of the fresh food stuffs and all of that virgin timber that is growing along the coast line."

Patty and Virginia glanced at each other. For the past several nights, they had talked away in their beds rather than going right to sleep. Either Virginia would come to Patty's bed or Patty would go to Virginia's. They would talk about the latest fashion styles that women in California wore, or they supposed they did. The women in New York wore beautiful clothes and New York had a huge harbor and shipping business. Steamboats brought some of the luxurious clothes to them, and they were sure they would soon be near a hub of activity. They had admired the pictures of beautiful parasols and hats. They had marveled at how people talked with such enthusiasm about the exotic port of San Francisco and the bigger city of Sacramento. Ships from Europe sailed into the San Francisco Bay bringing the fancy clothes, new ideas, and beautiful furniture. They had read of these in *The Living Age* and *The Town and Country* magazines that their father had brought home. *Now we would be able to visit the great city*, Patty thought to herself as she finished her milk.

Eliza brought in two large fruit pies and set them on the long sideboard. When she started clearing the dishes, Patty and Virginia got up to help her.

"Life on the journey will be just like it is here. Eliza will cook and Milt here has agreed to drive the oxen. We'll take everything we want. I'll build the biggest and best wagon so you can ride in comfort, Mrs. Keyes. You'll see, you'll travel across the prairies and mountains in the most luxurious and comfortable wagon ever tethered to a team of oxen."

Sarah smiled fondly at her son-in-law. He was a good man and took care to make sure she was always comfortable and included her in all of the family matters. She was certain that with his excellent carpentry skills, he would build a beautiful wagon. He ran a very successful furniture business here in Springfield and of course he would be able to do the same in the California territory.

"Can we really take the dogs?" Patty asked tentatively, looking at Tommy.

"Oh yes! We must bring my dog, Cash," cried Tommy. "As I said, he will protect us. Of course, Tyler must come too."

"Yes, all of the dogs will come to help us make our new home. Now," looking like the concerned father he was, he regarded everyone at the table and said, "I want you to think about this move very carefully. Give it some thought. Shall we all vote later this evening?"

Everyone was smiling and continued eating the berry pie slices on their plates. With the conclusion of dinner, plates and glasses were cleared.

Patty and Virginia hugged each other. Then it was real! They had talked with their mother and had decided if Milt would drive the oxen, then they would go to California. Everyone loved Milt. He had worked for their father in one of his furniture-making stores. But his talents did not end there. He could ride, rope, shoe, and drive horses, mules, and oxen. He was a man they could all depend upon, and he had become a close friend of the family. They could not think about taking the trip without either their beloved grandmother or Milt.

That evening, Patty helped her sister and Eliza wash the dishes. Working away in the cozy kitchen, there was more excited chatter about the vote that evening and the possible move out west.

"It would be such an adventure!" Eliza exclaimed. "I have lived here all my life."

"Maybe you'll find yourself a husband out there," Virginia said but immediately regretted it.

Patty looked at Eliza, who did not seem to care about Virginia's statement. *Poor Eliza*, Patty mused. She was plain but was such a sweet woman. She was an excellent cook, but for some reason, she didn't have much luck with the men around Springfield. She didn't have a beau that Patty knew of. Then, there was also Bayliss. Bayliss was Eliza's brother. He was a good-looking, pale, and sometimes sickly young man. There was something not quite right about him. He was quiet and often could not keep up with an average conversation. He did not live on his own but with his sister. Eliza loved him so much. She had been looking after him since they were children. *Maybe that was why she hadn't married*, Patty was thinking. She looked at Virginia and Eliza.

Virginia caught a glimpse of herself in the glass on the sideboard. Her hair was long, thick, and dark. Even at the age of thirteen, people noticed her and said she was pretty and petite. She smiled at her reflection. She was glad she was pretty, and she knew she was even prettier when she smiled. She saw Patty watching her. She smiled at her half-sister. Patty smiled back at her. Patty knew that what made her sister smile most were her family and her pony, Billy. She loved to ride and Patty thought she was the best girl rider in Springfield. She very often accompanied her father when he rode. They made a handsome pair, Mr. Reed on his huge gray mare, Glaucus, and Virginia on her fine pony. Billy was from famous racing stock and was a prized animal. Patty enjoyed watching Virginia wash and brush Billy. She loved her pony and she was quite proud to have her own. She was the only girl that she knew of with such a possession. It was a special privilege for her and she knew it.

Watching Virginia, Patty marveled at how they all resembled each other although Virginia was the most beautiful. Virginia's father died when she was an infant and when her mother remarried, James Reed raised Virginia as his own daughter. Being the oldest, she had always been the oldest girl, the oldest sister.

Patty had dark hair too, which she wore short. She also had wide-set, sparkling eyes. Where Virginia was vivacious and impetuous, Patty was calming, sweet, and responsible. She had keen intelligence and an immediate rapport with people. She cared deeply about people and loved her family fiercely. Although she was the younger of the daughters, Mrs. Reed often left the care of the younger boys in Patty's competent hands. The two girls were best friends and confidants no matter the five-year difference in their ages.

Virginia looked at Eliza hoping her words had not hurt her.

If Eliza took offense, she did not show it. "Maybe I will find me a Californian, maybe a cowboy or a naval officer." She winked at Virginia. "Do you think my time may have come? Maybe you will find a beau as well."

Virginia blushed and looked down at her dishtowel thinking thirteen was too young to think about marriage although she sometimes wondered what it would be like to have her own home and children. Thirteen was close to fourteen and most girls she knew were married by sixteen, so maybe it wasn't too early to think about it. She looked at Eliza, whipped her towel into a tight spiral, and was about to snap her towel at Eliza's backside when her mother came into the kitchen. Virginia straightened up, whipping the towel behind her back. She could feel her face turning red, and she sheepishly looked down.

"All done with the dishes?" her mother asked ignoring the flurry of towel play. They nodded. "Well, very well, and thank you. We are all meeting by the hearth." She led them into the large living area and to the grouping of chairs by the huge fireplace. A cheerful fire crackled. The room felt warm and inviting.

In front of the fireplace, several chairs surrounded a ruby-red rug. A footstool with intricate stitching made by Grandmother Keyes stood on its three legs by one side of the massive hearth. Velvet-topped chairs and two other straight-backed ones, which matched the ottoman, made a comfortable circle.

The girls joined the others in the living room. Patty sat on the ottoman, while Virginia spread herself on the floor. Eliza followed Patty bringing a tray of fragrant, hot apple cider. After passing out the mugs to all, she joined the group.

"Everyone has one vote to cast. Vote to go to California—or to not go." Mr. Reed looked around the room expectantly. "You too, Eliza. If you'd like to join us, you have a vote that counts as well. I understand your brother has agreed to go with us if you choose to go with us. Is that correct?" Eliza nodded and went to sit in a vacant chair.

"Well then, are we ready to vote? All those in favor of moving to the California Territory, raise your hand."

All around the circle, lighted by the gentle fire glow, each person raised their hands except for little Tommy who leaned against his mother in the overstuffed chair.

Tommy yawned and said, "I go with Jimmy and Patty." Everyone laughed.

"Of course you will, Tommy," said Patty bending down to pick him up and kiss him. He smiled and put his thumb in his mouth. He rested his head on her shoulder. With one thumb in his mouth and with his other hand, he twirled his hair. Then he raised his hand.

It was unanimous. The Reeds with Eliza, her brother, and Milt were going out west.

"It looks like we're moving to the golden shores of the Pacific!" Milt exclaimed.

In a sudden and unusual display of emotion, James Frazier Reed, who was conscious of his class and station in life and often acted like an aristocrat, grabbed his wife around her waist and twirled her around. "Maggie, my dear," he exclaimed, "we are off on our second honeymoon!" He kissed her on her reddened cheek as she protested modestly.

"Jim, not in front of the children," she said smoothing her satin skirt as she righted herself. Patty loved how her father showed affection to her mother.

"You'll see," he promised, "the mild Californian climate will be just what the doctor ordered. You'll be feeling fit as a fiddle every day starting with the journey." He looked deeply into her eyes, his brow knitted in concern thinking about her health. It had not been long ago that they had buried their son. Since then, Margaret had been prone to headaches, nausea, and sleeplessness. *Maybe the change would do her good*, he thought.

Margaret smiled and patted his cheek. He turned and winked at the girls. "We have months to get ready, but everyone should start planning. In no time at all, we will be loading the wagon and hitching the oxen."

That night when Patty went out to feed the dogs, she sat on the steps and announced, "You're moving with us." Cash, the family favorite, wolfed down his food and sat down beside her. She scratched the soft, brown fur behind his ears.

Tyler, Barney, Trailer, and Tracker were the other dogs, but they were working dogs. They went out every day and worked the cows and oxen. Little Cash usually stayed at home or went with the group when Virginia ventured out on her pony.

"You shall sleep with me and keep me warm." She squeezed Cash closer to her. Both of them sat on the porch watching the other dogs finish their supper and then check each other's bowls, giving a lick here and there, to make sure they were empty as well. Little Cash licked her on her cheek.

"It will be an adventure," she promised the little dog, "one we shall never forget."

After the girls were dressed in their nightclothes, they slipped into their grandmother's room. Patty followed Virginia as they entered her sleeping chamber.

Grandmother was sitting back on several feather pillows in her four-poster bed. "Come girls." She patted her bed. "Come sit beside me. What topic shall we talk about tonight?" She smiled to herself as if there were other topics. "Shall we talk more about the coming trip or something else?"

"Indians!" both girls chorused.

Nodding, she smiled. "I thought so. Now that you know you will be meeting Indians, you might pay more attention to the details. Now where was I?"

"Your Aunt had been playing outside and not paying attention to her Mother calling her," Patty began.

"Then she was captured by Savages who took her back to their tribe. It was an early settlement in Kentucky and Indians were always attacking the settlers," added Virginia. As she talked, Virginia slowly scooted her back to the headboard of the bed. The headboard was secured to the wall. She checked behind her one more time as she settled her back flush securely against the wood, perhaps to make sure no savage might be standing over her, tomahawk in hand, ready to attack her.

"Maybe you *were* paying attention," Grandmother said. "Life as a captive was very difficult and lonely for my aunt. They spoke only a few words of English and she had to work hard to learn their language. She had to learn to obey them and tried very hard to please them because she was afraid they would kill her otherwise. She worked very hard to be considered a strong member of the family she lived with. She learned to ride bareback. She could kill, clean, and cook wildlife. All the time she was held captive, she missed her family. She imagined ways she might escape, but it took five years until she could carry out her plan." The girls never tired of hearing about the kidnapping of their grandmother's aunt, her life among the savages, and her eventual escape.

They said their good nights, kissed their grandmother, and then scuttled off to bed holding hands as they climbed the stairs. Dark shadows moved stealthily outside the reach of the flicker of the candle. The flame wavered back and forth as Patty carried the candlestick. Patty stopped. Virginia turned to her in alarm.

"What is it?" she hissed, thinking Indians could even be in Springfield.

"I'm going down for Cash."

"You about made my heart give out!" she gasped, clutching her chest.

"I'm sorry, Dear Puss." Patty smiled and put her hand tenderly to her cheek. "Go on to bed and I'll be up shortly with our protector."

That night, as she did most nights, Patty tiptoed quietly downstairs and opened the door. "Cash," she called softly into the night. "Here, Cash, come on, boy. Oh, there you are." She smiled as he ran up the porch steps. The other dogs looked up as she opened the doors, but they didn't get up to join the smaller dog. Instead, they each curled up into tight little circles and laid their heads down. Cash sat at her feet and looked up. "Now be quiet." She held her index finger to her lips. He cocked his head to the left. "Come on then, sshhh…" They quickly went up the stairs after Patty made sure no one was in the foyer. She missed the shadowy figure in the darkened corner.

Emerging from those shadows, her mother smiled as she watched Patty bring the dog into the house and sneak him upstairs. She shook her head silently, gently confirmed the cross latch on the door was secure, and, still smiling, went back into the living room. Her girls were safe. She turned down the light from the kerosene lamp and proceeded upstairs. Halfway up the stairs, she paused and looked at the picture of the young smiling face of a baby boy. Her baby boy now dead and gone. She lost herself in the dark, happy eyes. That was before his eyes became pale and listless. Before he didn't laugh any more. Before they buried him in the cold, hard ground with the November sky threatening to rain again. "Cry with me," she had agonized to the skies. Shaking her fist, she repeated, "Cry with me as I bury my baby one month before his first year birthday." She hadn't wanted the day to be nice as she said her goodbyes to her little one. She wanted the sky to cry with her. Touching the handkerchief to her eyes she kissed her fingers and touched his cherubic laughing face on the picture, said goodnight, and continued going slowly upstairs to bed.

Chapter Two

The Preparations for the Move Begin in Earnest, 1846

The next morning, as the children went out to do their chores, their parents sat in the sitting room discussing what they would need to bring with them. They had already gathered several lists made available to any emigrant planning to join a wagon train.

"There is so much to do. I don't know if I can get it all together before we go, Jim." Mrs. Reed looked doubtful.

"You'll get it all done and then some, Maggie. Remember, all of us will help. You will get it done. We have four months."

Margaret reflected on the things that needed to be done. Lists of provisions had to be compiled making sure there would be enough for everyone. They would need food to feed seven people, a team of oxen, dogs, horses, and a cow. Bags of grain were stockpiled in the barn. The root vegetables were dug up and stored in the cellar under the house. They would need to furrow their crop lands to make ready for the new owners. The trees would be budding with fruit soon. What a shame that most of the fruit would not be eaten by them except for the apples which they had harvested and they could store.

"We'll need about 200 pounds of grain per person," James told Margaret.

Margaret nodded. "I'll add cornmeal, and we'll need soda and yeast for biscuits and bread. We'll need salt, rice, crackers, and of course a goodly supply of hardtack. We will start the trip with freshly picked berries and vegetables. We can dry some more before the winter ends and take it with us. You did say we would be in California before the winter, right? I think we'll butcher a pig before we go. How long will it take to reach the new territory?"

"Most groups take three to four months, but some had traveled more quickly. They are all settled and building new homes by the fall season."

"That sounds good."

"You are setting out a good list; we'll have three wagons to distribute the weight. I have completed building the first and largest of our wagons. They should be ready to load a few weeks before we leave."

"Good, because we'll also need tea, coffee, maple sugar, and vinegar. We'll smoke a side of beef before we go."

Jim nodded appreciatively at his wife.

"And I'll make up a batch of my pickles before we go too," Eliza added as she carried a tray of coffee and hot cobbler in for the Reeds.

Mrs. Reed smiled and added pickles to her list. "Good, what else?"

"We will need food that travels well."

"We should take some of the canned goods from the Mercantile. Then we can have some of those special treats whenever we want. Since they are so expensive, it will be nice to have them for sharing with some of the other wagons," Margaret said, lengthening her list. She was so pleased with the availability of tin cans. A rather new invention, she remembered. They had been able to buy tins for about a decade now. Being able to eat peaches in the winter was quite a treat. "Now, we do plan to be there by late fall? I don't want to end up the last few days in the snow."

"Silly Maggie, no!" James exclaimed, cutting an extra helping of cobbler. "You can count on celebrating Thanksgiving in our new home."

Margaret smiled at him, and Eliza gave a little two-step dance as she went back to the kitchen.

"We will need a lot of other items as well," Mr. Reed continued.

There were other staples and items to bring. Many letters had been circulated by settlers who had preceded them. They would need knives, an ax, a hatchet, a spade, a saw, scissors, needles, thread, ropes, cotton cloth, soap, candles, tallow, a spyglass, lanterns, a washbowl, a camp stool, and spare parts for the wagons. It was a fact that the wagons would need constant repair. They would also have to assemble and disassemble them according to the terrain. They would have to mend the leathers, the harnesses, and other riggings. The list grew longer and longer, but with three wagons, the Reeds felt confident they could carry everything, and the weight should not cause their oxen undue suffering.

Scrutinizing her lists, which had grown to several pages, Mrs. Reed sat back and put a hand to her forehead. She closed her eyes and rested her head against her rocker. Her husband leaned forward.

"Are you having one of your headaches?"

"No," she lied, smiled, and patted his hand. "I'm doing fine."

Patty came down the stairs and listened at the doorway as her parents discussed the trip.

"It will be very difficult for Mother Keyes," her father was saying. His dark eyebrows knitted into a frown. "I am not sure I like the idea of her or you in one of those wagons. I do worry about you."

Margaret nodded her head. "I know you do. I also worry about mother, but me? I shall be fine. I am feeling much better and I am much stronger recently."

His hand caressed her arm. "Although it should be an easy journey, it will be a long one. Maybe we should try to talk her into staying. Your brothers certainly want her to stay here."

"Yes, but she is pretty insistent that she stays with her only daughter. And you know how we Keyes women can be, don't you now, Mr. James Frazier Reed?" Margaret flashed a smile at him and he smiled and nodded in return. "Anyway, if we can get her comfortably to Fort Hall, she can stay with my brother Robert until she feels well enough to travel to be with us. He's been three long years in the Oregon Territory, and she misses him mightily."

"She has to come with us!" declared Patty. She pushed off

the doorway and walked to stand by her father. "You have to do something, Pa. You know if there is anything I can do, I'll do it. I can stay here with her too." Patty had thought long and hard about the possibility of staying with her frail grandmother. Possibly, she would keep her youngest brother with them and join her parents at a later time.

It is so like of dear Patty to miss the excitement of the trip to the California Territory to stay and care for her grandmother, thought Jim Reed.

"We'll find a way for wonderful Grandmother Keyes to make the trip in total comfort," vowed her father. "Then you can make the journey with us."

Although he had told his wife about the first huge wagon being completed, he did not tell Patty about the fine wagon he had built. He would keep his word.

"Do something" he certainly did. Owning a furniture business and being a furniture maker himself, he had a super wagon made. It stood almost two stories tall. The typical Conestoga wagon had openings at the front and back and they were covered by white wagon canvases. Virginia named the wagon, "The Palace," but others not so enamored with the elegant title called it the Reed wagon. Boasting a side entrance with steps, the wagon had two stories. Instead of hard, flat bench seats, there were spring seats used in the best stage-coaches. The "first floor" carried a stove complete with a pipe opening through the roof for smoke. There was a table, chairs, Mrs. Reed's sideboard, a hutch, a small table for the kitchen, a cupboard, a dresser, a wardrobe, and two beds. The "second floor" housed the children's beds and several canvas bags of clothes and linens. There was space under the "first floor" for pots, pans, cooking implements, tools, and hardware for the horses and oxen. Several favorite books they had collected would go with them in a small library. There was even a mirror by the side door so the ladies could check their dresses and coiffures as they left and entered the wagon.

The next stop was to go to the Mercantile in Springfield.

Virginia and Patty were fitted for new dresses, while Jimmy and little Tom were fitted for shirts of Linsey-woolsey, a durable and practical material of twilled cotton made for long wear and comfortable travel clothing. The boys especially liked the red flannel shirts. The girls like the striped cotton twill and the calico that added color. There were lace collars for the girls and pieces of fur to make collars for the winter wear.

Patty and Virginia felt like queens while they were in town gathering material, ribbons, lace, and other notions. The whole town was talking about their imminent departure.

"You'll be the talk of the town, you two. How big is San Francisco, or is it Sacramento?" Mrs. Potter, the shop mistress, wanted to know.

"Won't we, though!" exclaimed Virginia curtsying with a bolt of sunflower yellow wrapped around her. The bright color favored her dark hair. For a moment, her mother thought she looked like a china doll.

"We don't know how big the towns are, but people talk about them," Margaret answered. "I think Sacramento is quite small and Sutter's Fort is the main area. Do you have some yellow satin hair ribbons?"

"I think these would go nicely," Mrs. Potter declared holding up some glossy yellow ribbons to Virginia's hair.

"Oh, Ma, they are lovely!" declared Patty coming over to stroke the ribbons. "They are perfect, aren't they Ginny?"

Virginia nodded happily and hugged her mother. "Oh, they are so lovely. Thank you."

"Now," said Margaret tapping her cheek, "let's see about that periwinkle blue for Patty."

"Oh Mother, could we?" Patty danced around her mother.

"Yes, you will need a good dance dress. If I am not mistaken, we'll have many a beau come a courtin' this winter. Why, when they see your sister..."

"I'm not going to no dance," interjected Jimmy who had tagged along on the shopping excursion. "There is no way I am going to no dance."

"I'm not going to *any* dance," corrected Patty, "and no, you don't have to, dear brother." She then hugged Jimmy. "We'll be fine going by ourselves."

Patty thought about the thrill of going to an adult dance while Virginia thought about all the new boys she would meet. She dreamed of being the 'belle of the ball' and choosing one special boy. This trip would be the adventure of her life!

After Mrs. Potter wrapped the purchases in brown paper and tied them with string, she said, "You'll have enough for three or four new dresses for the girls, shirts for the boys and Mr. Reed, and a few dresses for yourself, Mrs. Reed. I think the Periwinkle blue would make a lovely dress for you too."

"I thank you for your time and help, Mrs. Potter. We shall miss your mercantile. I hear the availability of goods and stores at Sutter's Fort and other California cities are not as bountiful as it is here in Springfield."

"Well, we do have the reputation for miles around here, but I am sure you will find good shopkeepers out in the new territory. This supply will last you a good while until you are ready for new clothes again."

All chorused, "Thank you again," as they left the store. The girls were excited as they twirled out of the store and Margaret paused for a moment and felt a welling in her chest. This was good-bye. How she loved to come into town and shop. She had so many friends in the shopkeepers. *Oh well, she thought, I guess I will be making new friends and finding new shops to buy our things in.* She checked to make sure they had all of their bundles, then they headed home.

Mrs. Potter watched the Reed family disappear down the street. The Reeds and the Donners had been the subject of many discussions. It amazed their friends and acquaintances that they were attempting this huge move. Why, just the other day she and her husband were talking with their neighbors.

"Why would someone as well off as James Frasier Reed or even the Donner brothers want to leave Springfield?" asked Mr. Potter.

"Not only that," answered their neighbor, "but California belongs to Mexico. Right now, Mexico is arguing with the United States over Texas and who rightly owns the land. I don't think the Mexican government is going to like so many people from the United States coming in and setting up homesteads in their country. It isn't safe."

Mrs. Potter shook her head as she remembered their conversation. It was all well and good for James Reed and George and Jacob Donner to go to the new territory, but to uproot and take their wives and children too did not seem quite right. What with Mrs. Keyes being so old and feeling so poorly? And what about sweet little Tamsen Donner? She was just a mite of a person. Moreover, Mrs. Reed had just finished burying her little boy. She did not seem strong enough for this endeavor. Oh, how she would miss them and their business! And how she would worry about them! They would be kept close in her prayers.

* * * * *

The days of preparation soon came to a close.

The Reed party included a total of three wagons, the large one for the family and the other two for those who accompanied them and for the food and supplies. The additional members were Eliza, her half-brother Bayliss Williams, and Milton Elliott. Two other men joined Milt as teamsters for the other two wagons; they were James Smith and Walter Heron.

Eliza was happy her brother wanted to come. They were hoping to cash in on the new good life of the territories. It was time that life dealt them some better cards. Bayliss wasn't like other men. Although they were close in age, he did not have the ability to think things through clearly and often depended upon Eliza to take care of him. Oh, he could do simple things and follow directions, but he wasn't good at starting things that he thought of himself. She sighed when she thought of him and figured he would always be with her. That was fine, but it would be easier if they had their own land. Then they could have their own home and place for farming. They would start a brand new life.

Eliza was also pleased that Mr. Reed had said they were meeting up with another group of people. The Donners had put together a group of people who also wanted to go west. This would make a large wagon train. She would feel safer with the larger group of people. Mr. Reed was such a powerful and commanding man, Eliza wasn't bothered that he could be difficult. Although she believed that strong men were often more difficult to live with, it suited her that Mr. Reed was well off and was an important man in the community.

Chapter Three

The Reed and Donner families leave for California – Springfield, Illinois to Fort Laramie, Wyoming, April 14, 1846

What excitement that April day brought when the Reeds and the two Donner families left Springfield! Several friends and family had come to see them off. The wagons were loaded with furniture, food, clothes, dishes, silver pieces, and silverware.

The night before, on April 13th, the two Donner families had driven six wagons into Springfield so everyone would be ready to leave in the morning. There was a noisy crowd. Friends and relatives all came out to wish them well and to see them off. The atmosphere was festive with barking dogs, laughing children, women wearing their best Sunday dresses and hats. Even the men had spiffed up to see this momentous wagon train depart.

Nine wagons left Springfield that morning. Every wagon had the family name painted on the side. All the Donners joined the Reeds. Each family had three wagons and the group numbered 31. The largest and most beautiful wagon, built by James Reed, was the "The Palace Wagon," so nicknamed by Virginia Reed. Oxen pulled them all; large wooden yokes linked each pair of oxen. Each yoke of two oxen were counted as one. The "Palace" was pulled by four yoke of oxen. "That is eight oxen!" exclaimed Patty. "We have the biggest and the most beautiful home on wheels."

Behind the Palace on a lead line was the family milk cow. Virginia and Patty had trouble deciding which of the mild-mannered milk cows they would take with them. The beautiful brown cow Daisy won out, and she walked contentedly behind the wagon.

Grandma Keyes was carried out to the Palace Wagon by James.

She was wrapped in her down comforter looking very small and frail. Patty solicitously followed her father out as he placed Mrs. Keyes gently in her feather bed, the one he had spent extra hours on to make as comfortable for her as he could. "Oh, my!" she exclaimed. "This is just like my bedroom. Thank you, Jim, this is very nice."

Patty went to sit on the bed with her.

The last few items were lifted aboard. Finally, they were ready.

The huge crowd quieted down.

James Reed and Jacob Donner mounted their horses. Each wagon's driver held up the reins. Women and children sat on wagon seats or inside the wagons.

"Everyone mounted and ready?" shouted James. "Then let's go to the fertile lands of the new territories!" A loud shout came from both inside and outside of the wagons. This was it; they were starting their new destiny. Slowly, like a languid snake, the small wagon train began to move forward. The town's people and relatives of the Reeds walked or rode alongside the wagons. Many would camp out with them the first night and many uncles of James and Margaret Reed continued on with them for the first several days.

"Look, Grandma," said Patty excitedly holding up the heavy canvas so she could watch as their hometown grew smaller and smaller. "I'll hold this up so you can watch the whole town say goodbye."

As the town became a speck behind them, Patty got up and walked to the front of the wagon. She did not even have to balance herself against the furniture as she walked inside, she marveled at how smooth the going was. She peeked out the front to where Tommy and Jimmy were sitting beside Milton on the wooden bench seat. Tommy sat close to Jimmy. They both kept their eyes on the oxen, because everyone knew you could not trust oxen.

Milt smiled down at the boys. He lifted his right arm up and flicked the tip of his whip down yelling, "Yaw!" The oxen increased their pace.

Virginia clucked at her pony, Billy, urging him to keep up with her father. He cut such a dashing figure on Glaucus, his fine horse. The mare's soft, gray coat cast a velvet-like sheen over her withers. Her father sat tall in the saddle, his dark hair, hatless, ruffled gently by the breeze. Looking very much the aristocrat, he led the small wagon train. She rode faster and caught up with him.

Her yellow and orange calico dress with its wide skirt made riding easy. Her bonnet hung from the ties around her neck onto her back. The colors of her bonnet stood out against her dark hair streaming down her back. She knew people from the wagon train commented as she rode by with her father. They always did. It was an unusual occurrence for her, a young girl, to have her own horse. Moreover, it was unusual that she was riding and not walking or riding in the wagons. But Virginia was a fine horsewoman. She had several ribbons and prizes she had won from county fairs for her riding. These prizes she had tucked in her canvas bag of clothing.

Virginia loved Billy and felt free riding. Even though she was 13, she had been riding for years. She often accompanied her father in riding about Springfield. She would miss Springfield, the fine shops, and the beautiful dresses. Virginia was quite petite; what with her dark hair and porcelain white skin, she looked like an artist's drawings in the catalogs! She caught up with her father. It would not be long before she was in Sacramento trying on the latest fashions from Europe.

They came to the first bridge. Virginia reined in Billy. She looked back at the wagons. She knew the oxen could have trouble crossing the bridge. They might fall off the bridge dragging the wagon with them. It was the first water crossing; she felt a clutch in her stomach. She made her decision. "I need to go back to our wagon," she called out to her father. He smiled and nodded. She trotted back quickly.

Milt had stopped the wagon, and the children clambered out. Jimmy, Tommy, and Patty gave the wagon wide berth.

"Wait, wait!" Virginia cried, riding up to the wagon. All the children knew about the possible impending danger that came with driving the oxen. With only heavy yokes on and no reins or bridles, they knew the oxen could move about on their own whim. They could walk along the side of the bridge and misstep, and the heavy wooden yoke, the oxen, and then the wagon could fall into the water. "Make sure the oxen don't miss the bridge, and don't forget Grandma is in the back of the wagon!" she cried.

Milt tilted his head back and laughed. Repositioning his hat, he flicked his whip and the oxen clambered up and onto the bridge. *Miss the bridge!* He chuckled to himself. "There is no way these beasts will miss the bridge. I declare you young'uns have the oddest notions. Miss the bridge." He laughed again long and loudly.

Patty held Tommy and Jimmy's hands as they walked behind the wagon over the bridge. The three kept alert just in case something happened.

"You certainly know how to make them behave the whip, Mr. Elliott," declared Virginia.

"Thank you, Miss Virginia. I have been driving oxen since I was a young sprout." He didn't add that there were going to be many treacherous times when the oxen would be difficult to drive. They'd "cross that bridge when they came to it."

She nodded and urged Billy to catch up with her father and her uncle at the lead of the wagon train.

"So, you've come to ride with me and Uncle Jake," her father said smiling as she rode up.

The three rode on ahead leading the wagons towards Nebraska's Platte River. They followed the way of the Kansas River to the Little Blue River which then intersected with the Platte and continued North to the North Platte River and onto Fort Laramie.

Patty was walking along with George Jr. and Mary Donner. They were Uncle Jake's children. George was nine and Mary was seven. They liked to walk in the morning before they got tired or bored. Often running ahead to walk out in front of the first wagon, they stayed behind the lead horsemen. When walking up in front, they were subject to less dust. Then later in the afternoon, they liked to ride in the wagons. If they were in the "Palace," they would play games or draw. If they were in Uncle George's wagon, Aunt Tamsen would read to them or let them look at her books. Aunt Tamsen had brought many of her books with her. She was planning to continue teaching when they arrived in the new territories. In Uncle Jake's wagon, they would play board games.

"Now watch carefully for Indians. Remember if you see them, call out. We are to go to the nearest wagon and climb in. It is not for us to keep walking and find out if they are friendly or not," Patty warned them.

"I'll just die if I see an Indian," Mary claimed.

"Well, you will see many along the trail. We must stay alert and be very quiet when we do see them." George looked sharply at his sister and said, "No silly screaming."

"I wouldn't scream," retorted Mary a little uncertainly, "but they better not surprise me!"

"I thought that is what they do, they sneak up on you," said Patty. Little Cash was walking by her side. She liked it when he stayed with them. Sometimes, he would run up in front with the other four dogs walking with the lead horse riders. Then he would come back and fall in step with Patty. He was having a grand time with the other dogs trotting alongside the wagons. It worried Patty, too. She was worried about the Indians and about having the dogs on the trail. She had heard the men talking about the dogs. They had discussed the merits of having dogs with them as well as the problems.

"The dogs will bark and warn the Indians that we are near," Uncle Jake had said.

"True," admitted James, "and they will also bark and let us know if the Indians are sneaking into camp at night. And they will also bark and scare the Indians." They had decided to wait and see if the dogs would be a liability. Patty was sure the dogs would be good company and guards for the wagons.

"Indians often suddenly appear," said George, intruding on Patty's thoughts bringing her back to the conversation with George and Mary. "Sometimes they ride right up to you and want to trade."

"Yes, and we have things to trade with the Indians," Mary said. They all nodded because, as they packed, they brought along trinkets and things they thought they could trade with the Indians.

The three lapsed into silence, each preoccupied with their own thoughts. The feelings of tension and fear mounted mixed with the excitement around the probability that they would soon see Indians. The reputation of the Indians was fearful. This was the territory of the Pawnee, the Snake, and the Sioux. Each group was considered a fierce and warlike group. They were not known to be friends with the white men who more and more frequently marched into their homelands. Many a raiding party stole animals and kidnapped or killed the pioneers as they moved in never-ending waves to the west. It wouldn't be long before they encountered them. Would they be friendly, or were they the savages the settlers had been warned about?

The sun was high overhead and had already started its march to the right across the sky. The wagons came to a stop. They let the cattle, oxen, and horses drink water and graze. Those riding inside got out of the wagons to eat. Others completed chores before joining the group for the midday meal.

The women brought out bread, slabs of beef, cheese, and fresh butter. They drank water and milk. Patty or Virginia milked the cow every morning. The fresh milk was delightful and gave them cream and butter. That morning, Patty had given Eliza a large bowl of milk. Eliza had separated the cream to churn into butter while they were rumbling over the prairie. She had set out a covered bucket, and the rocking and jostling of the wagon had done the chore of churning.

"This is the life," declared Uncle Jake. He stretched out pretending to yawn and pantomiming that he was going to sleep.

The children giggled. Little Cash promptly got up and then lay against him using his leg as a pillow.

"Well, I guess this is a dog's life, too," he laughed, petting the head lying on his thigh.

A gentle breeze ruffled through the grasses. Long waves undulated gently for as far as they could see. They had left the woods for the most part and now traveled along good roads. Before them, on either side of the road, as far as the eye could see, were miles and miles of grassland. Off in the distance, they could see black dots–those would be buffalo grazing.

"Will you collect buffalo chips for our fires tonight?" Mother Reed asked the group of children sitting cross-legged eating thick slabs of bread with butter and cheese.

Leanne wrinkled her nose and the others nodded yes. Buffalo chips were the animals' droppings.

"It will be easy to fill the basket today!" exclaimed George. "They must have come through here a day or two ago."

"I'll leave the basket on the step of the porch here and you can drop them in as you collect them," Eliza said.

When they finished eating, Patty, Eliza, and Mary cleaned up and put away the remains of their meal. Virginia, Elitha, and Leanna rounded up the younger children, got them washed up, cleaned, and readied to move on. Elitha Donner was the most patient and tended to be the one the younger children looked up to and wanted to mind. Leanna Donner was her sweet-faced sister.

"Lewis and Tommy," she fussed, "my goodness, look at the mess you have made with that blackberry jam! Look at Samuel, just a year older and just as messy. Isaac, where is your hat?"

Lewis looked at his clean hand and promptly stuck his thumb into his mouth. Elitha chattered on good-naturedly to her charges and Virginia and Leanna helped her out.

"I am thinking we'd enjoy some nice buffalo steaks for breakfast. What do you think?" Patty's father asked the group.

"Oh, we'd love some, Mr. Reed," said Elitha enthusiastically.

"Oh yes," chorused Patty and Mary.

"I think I'll do just that. I will go out with a couple of the men and we will bring back some buffalo! What do you reckon, Milt? I'd say that herd is about ten to twenty miles out?"

"I'd say that'd be 'bout right," said Milt scratching his chin. "Think you can manage going out that way without me?"

"Oh, I guess I might be able to scare up some steaks with Bayliss and some of the other boys. Think you can manage the trail without me leading you?"

Milt laughed loudly looking at the wide, smooth road leading across the prairie. "Hope you make it back tonight. Eliza says she's baking bread to go with the fresh churned butter. I'm not sure there will be any left tomorrow morning."

"I would hope there would be a crust left for this mighty hunter. Be a shame if I were too weak from hunger to go out and hunt again." Both men laughed at the absurdity of the idea.

Mr. Reed turned his horse and went down the line of wagons looking for a few volunteers to go with him after the buffalo. He passed Patty walking back towards one of the Donner wagons with her apron full of greens and wild flowers. She joined her mother and the other girls who were visiting with Tamsen.

"Aunt Tamsen, look what I have collected for you." Patty laid out several bunches of wildflowers.

Tamsen Donner bent over the fragrant and vividly colored collection of flowers. "Oh my, these are lovely, Patty. Let's see what you have found. Here is a wild tulip, and look at the pink blush on this primrose."

"This one is a lupine," said Elitha picking up the purple-blue stalk. Each dark blossom clustered in tight formation climbing up the green stem. "I certainly like this color."

"What's this one called?" asked Mary picking up a large bunch of red and green blossoms. "They are so pretty."

"They are indeed a beautiful bloom and one I am not familiar with. It looks like the bloom of a beech tree, but I have never seen these colors." Tamsen Donner was sketching the blossoms as she spoke. "It is easier to draw them now. I can color them this evening. The jolting of the wagon makes it difficult, and tonight I'll be able to color the pictures in more carefully. Then I can look them up and see what they are."

"You can ride with me and mother, Tamsen," Margaret Reed offered. "I love to watch you draw and describe the plants and flowers we have been finding."

"I would enjoy visiting with you this afternoon. Elitha, would you put the children down to their naps and then walk alongside the wagon this afternoon?"

"Yes, Mama." Elitha enjoyed being responsible for her brother and sisters. It had been such a lovely trip so far. The weather was wonderful, the food plentiful, and the walk easy. Her siblings as well as the other children had been so easy to take care of because the trip had been so easy. It was going to be a wonderful trip to the western shores of California.

"I'll plan to come and draw and we can visit then, Margaret. How is your mother feeling today?"

"She says she is feeling pretty well today. She ate a hearty breakfast. Eliza skimmed off some of the cream from the milk this morning. I think it is good for her." Both women nodded. Mrs. Keyes was frail, but so far, she was holding her own.

It took no time to start up the wagons again moving forward. They only made fires when they made camp in the evening and, of course, in the morning before starting the day. They took nothing but food and drink out for their brief midday stop and water for the cattle and oxen. So after the lunch break, it was a matter of getting everyone situated for the afternoon trek.

The wagon train slowly moved forward while James Reed rode off with four younger men to hunt the buffalo.

"I can't wait until I am old enough to join the hunters," George Jr. stated.

Patty was not listening to George complain. "I'm going to ride in the wagon with Mother and Grandmother." She was becoming increasingly worried about her grandmother. She looked so fragile and pale. She seemed to be as pale as her porcelain dolly. And my goodness, she was so old. Patty ran alongside the Palace Wagon and easily swung up onto the side step. Mrs. Keyes was resting. Patty put her hand on her cheek and kissed her lightly.

Her grandmother opened her eyes and smiled at her granddaughter. *Patty is such a lovely and thoughtful granddaughter*, she thought. She reached out and patted her arm, closed her eyes, and went back to sleep.

"Come join us, Patty," said her mother, patting the space beside her on the bench. She nodded towards her resting mother. "Grandmother is having a rest after her lunch, which she enjoyed. So come sit with us." She and Tamsen were sitting by a wooden table. Tamsen had her drawings and descriptions of the plants and flowers they had been passing by. Many examples of the plants were also on the table.

Patty sat next to her and looked through the book. "I want to learn the names of all these plants, especially the flowers. Do you know the names of all of them?"

"Not all of them," laughed Tamsen, "I am still learning about them. Like the ones you brought me today. If you keep bringing me a pretty sample of any flower or plant that you see, I can draw them and name them and if I don't know the name, I can look them up in my books."

"Oh yes," said Patty, "I will keep collecting them and so will Jimmy, Virginia, Elitha, and Leanna. Will you teach me to draw too?"

"I will be happy to. We can set up a time and we can practice drawing and looking up all of the flora and fauna." Tamsen smiled down at Patty. How she loved teaching and how she missed her days in the schoolhouse. She hoped to start teaching again when they reached their destination. George had promised she would teach again. She planned on starting a school for girls.

"Are you really going to start a Ladies Seminary, Tamsen?" Margaret asked interrupting her thoughts.

"Yes," she laughed. "I was thinking of that very thing. I have about all I need to get started. I have brought so many books, tablets, and other necessary classroom items. When we are settled, I can buy the additional supplies that we will need. Some of the families can help get the school started as payment for their girls' lessons."

"Can I be one of your students, Aunt Tamsen?" Patty asked. "I do love to read, even more so than Virginia."

"I would most certainly like you to be one of my young ladies, Patty. I'd like to extend the invitation to Virginia as well. A lady needs to know her letters and be able to write a fine hand."

"How about some tea, ladies?" Eliza asked. She had stoked the iron stove with the buffalo chips the children had collected. The kettle was boiling with hot water.

"How lovely," said Tamsen as she sat back in her seat.

Eliza brought a tray with china cups and saucers, a tin of tea, fresh cream in a tiny porcelain pitcher that she had skimmed off the milk that Patty had gotten from their cow that morning. She also brought a dish of fresh butter from the rest of the cream which she churned that morning as well. She also had blackberry jam for the just-made biscuits she had taken from the stove. The warmth from the stove and smell of fresh biscuits was comforting.

"Oh, Eliza," sighed Tamsen as she bit into her biscuit. "Fresh butter, preserves, and biscuits. This trip has been lovely. The scenery has been beautiful."

"I am surprised the roads have been so easy to travel on," Margaret agreed. She looked over at her sleeping mother. "I truly appreciate the wide, easy road to travel on and I love these spring loaded seats!"

"Yes, and how clever of your husband to use the same seats they use in buggies! They make traveling a dream." Tamsen stretched back in her comfortable seat. She did not begrudge the Reeds their fancy wagon. Although the Donners were well-to-do like the Reeds, they did not have as much money as them. They did have a large amount of money, several thousand dollars, that Tamsen had secretly sewn into the quilt she kept on their bed. Her husband did not have as important of a position as James Reed; after all, there was a town named after Jim Reed. The Donners were well off and Tamsen was very comfortable with the life George was providing for her. Besides, Tamsen had her teaching and being a teacher fulfilled her.

Patty ate two biscuits with lots of butter and jam. Seeing that her grandmother was sleeping and she herself was getting bored listening to the women talk, she jumped up and kissed her mother.

"I am a-joining George and Mary," she sang out. Then she disappeared out the side entrance as quickly as she had come in. Tamsen had opened her mouth to correct her English, but Patty was gone.

"She is such a sweet girl, Margaret," Tamsen laughed. "Oh, that energy she has!"

"She and Virginia have been such great strength for me. They help me with Jimmy and Tommy, they help Eliza, and they both have been so considerate of Mother. I rely on them so." Margaret smiled at the side entrance where Patty had disappeared. She suddenly thought of the baby boy they had buried and left in Springfield. She took a deep breath and blinked her eyes. Tamsen glanced at her and noticed the pain in her eyes. Intuitively, she knew that Margaret was thinking of her son. She looked down at her drawing making a few more marks on the paper, giving Margaret some privacy to collect her thoughts.

The two women then chatted as Eliza came and cleared the tea things.

The nine wagons rumbled along. The trail was wide, easy, and not too dusty. The children walked, ran, and skipped alongside as their mothers walked and chatted. Margaret, Tamsen, and Eliza chatted about dinner plans and recipes. Tamsen would spot a plant or berry and send one of the kids out to collect it and then they would decide how to prepare it for the next meal, or save it for the following day.

They were beginning the dinner process that evening when the men came back from a successful hunt. The buffalo was dressed out and large steaks were carved and divided among all the wagons. After putting the fresh meat on the spit, everyone ate their fill of just cooked buffalo. Patty and Tommy took turns throwing the dogs huge chunks of meat. That evening, Patty and Virginia helped Eliza cut some of the meat into strips so they could make buffalo jerky. Eliza had set some aside in vinegar as well as in heavy salt to help with curing and preserving the meat. The rest were hung in long strips. "We'll put these out along the outside of the wagon tomorrow to dry. They should last quite a while." It took a long time to cut up and distribute the meat, so the typical evening's entertainment was postponed. They went to sleep with the larders full of fresh and prepared buffalo.

Before they were to start late that May morning, Eliza called out to Patty and Tommy who were sitting on the grass checking the spokes of the big wagon wheels for splinters, big gouges, and any obvious cracks. This careful checking of the wheel spokes helped maintain their strength. "Will you keep an eye out for buffalo berries?" she asked. "I have seen so many flowering buffalo berry bushes and now the berries should be bright red and ready to pick." She deposited some baskets on the step.

"Oh boy," said Tommy. "I love buffalo berry jam."

"Yes'm," answered Patty. She looked at her hands. She knew that when they did find the buffalo berries that picking them would prick her hands as the bushes always had so many thorns. However, the picking wouldn't be hard. The red berries stood out among the bright green leaves and the bushes were always as tall as she was, so getting to the berries would not be hard. Therefore, Patty got up and picked up the baskets Eliza had left at the opening of the Grand Palace wagon.

Eliza saw her and said, "If you can't fill up the basket, get some berries that are turning as well. I have enough sugar to sweeten the pot." She smiled as she turned back to putting her kitchen in order for the day's breakfast.

That morning, fresh buffalo steaks sizzled over the fire, wafting a mouth-watering fragrance throughout the camp, and then breakfast was served. The dogs ate their fill again. Then strips of meat were hung along the outsides of all nine wagons, and they swung back and forth as the wagon train moved forward for the day. The sun would help dry the meat and the movement of the wagon's progress would keep the bug count down. It was another easy day's walk along the prairie.

That evening, everyone was ready for a celebration. After another dinner of thick buffalo steaks, they gathered around one large fire, sang, and danced. Towards the end of the evening, when everyone said their goodnights, peaceful feeling of camaraderie filled their hearts. The Donners and the Reeds were good friends and they were glad to be in the Reed-Donner party. They were appreciative of the hunting and leadership skills of James Reed. Everyone believed they would have an easy journey and they would remain good friends.

A glorious sunrise saw the small wagon train starting out. While the wagons progressed towards the west, Eliza cut some remaining strips of meat to dry to make into buffalo jerky.

The children had collected buffalo chips, large grass filled droppings from the poop piles that the huge herd had left. Soon, all the wagons sported barrels lashed to the sides full of the chips; knowing when they left the prairie and moved into the desert, they would have fuel for fire.

The day progressed quickly. That evening, around the fire, Grandmother Keyes told stories of her childhood. She had a soft, gentle voice and the children leaned forward to hear her talk. She soon tired and with Patty's help, she clambered up into the great wagon. Her bed was piled high with quilts and a down pillow. It didn't take long before she was sleeping peacefully.

"What is it, dear?" asked Patty's mother as she saw her daughter looking hesitantly at her.

"I noticed Grandmother ate little for dinner."

"I'm worried too, little one. However, she gets up every day and is ready to go. She smiles so even though I know her bones must be hurting her. She says she is fine, but I think she becomes weaker every day despite what she tells us."

"Oh, Mama." Patty hugged her mother and buried her head into her chest. "I am so worried she won't make the whole trip with us."

Patty's mother stroked her head. "We all are worried. Nevertheless, we will continue to make it as comfortable as possible for her. You do know Patty that this trip is very hard on her. She has been unwell for so long. She may not complete this trip. It is not for us to say. Her health is in the Lord's hands now. You are being such a comfort to her. She loves you so."

"I love her too," Patty echoed. She started to say more as tears sprang to her eyes and she let her head rest on her mother's shoulder. They sat together for a while staring out into the darkness listening to regular breathing of Mrs. Keyes, the rustling of the oxen outside, and the sound waves of the crickets, their chorus rising and falling from all around them. Soon, all of the lanterns were extinguished and, in total darkness, they said good night and felt their way to bed.

As they continued their journey, more wagons joined the group and the Reed-Donner wagon train grew in size. Many families were making the long trek to California or Oregon. It was better to ask and join an existing wagon train. At night, the families enjoyed individual family fires as they ate their supper and then the whole group would gather around a community bonfire. Gossip and travel plans were swapped. So many people were going out west. Some of the wagons would stay together until they separated outside of Fort Laramie, some continuing on the Oregon Trail, others pushing on to California.

The grasses of the prairie continued to move in long, undulating, lazy waves. The colors shifting from green to yellow-green to almost silver as the wind rustled through the long, luxuriant stems. Patty and Tommy sat towards the back of the wagon mesmerized by the sea-like action of the fields. The trail was smooth and since it was not difficult for the oxen to pull, the children were allowed to ride for short distances. The wagon train meandered down towards a fairly wide and deep creek. Now they were making their way clear of the water.

Virginia jumped up appearing from nowhere, her eyes wide and her index finger to her lips. "Shhhh," she hissed. "Indians!" She climbed up into the wagon with her siblings. This was it. They had talked at length about the Indians and what would happen when they encountered them. All those stories of Indians that her grandmother had told her came flooding back. Virginia took a big breath and slowly let it go.

"Where?" gasped Tommy.

"Look, up there, coming down that bluff!" Her hand trembled as she pointed.

Sure enough, a small group of Indians, on their ponies, was making its way towards the wagon train.

"What should we do?" cried Patty in fear.

"We'll hide, be quiet, and wait for Pa and the other men to talk to them." Virginia's face was white and her hands shook as she covered the three of them with quilts. "Quiet now," she admonished. They sunk down low peeking out at the scene as it unfolded before them. Tommy whimpered and buried his head into Patty's arms. She patted his back and murmured what she hoped were comforting words. She was terrified herself. She looked for Jimmy and saw that he was sitting on the side of the bed with their grandmother. Patty put her index finger to her lips indicating that he should be quiet. Jimmy nodded back and Patty turned back to the drama unfolding before her outside of the wagon.

The Indians had followed them from Soldier's Creek. A small group had broken off from the wagon train. The 13 wagons were too big and moving too slowly for the rest of the group, so they had moved on ahead at a faster speed leaving the slower, bigger wagons to lumber on. At that moment, Patty was thinking, *the rest of the group was right. We are too slow and now the Indians are going to get us! The wagon train had come to a stop.*

"What are they saying? I can't hear them, can you?" asked Patty.

"Shush. I can't hear them with you prattling like a magpie," Virginia scolded.

She popped her head up and out so she could see over the backboard. She could see her father and some of the other men talking with the Indians. They kept talking for a long time. She could see the Indians gesturing at the prairie and the wagons. Her father seemed to be doing most of the talking. She started when he pointed at their wagon. She ducked her head down below the wagon side. Had they seen her? *My father would be angry if he saw us*, she thought. She grabbed Patty's hand.

"What's happening?" croaked Patty terrified by Virginia's quick movements.

"Hush. Don't move. I think they are coming here."

"Coming here?" she hissed. "Oh no, I…" Tommy gasped and she looked at his little scared face and bent to give his cheek a kiss. "It's all right," she said soothingly.

Virginia squeezed Patty's hand harder. Both girls held their breath.

Nothing happened; they strained to hear the men talking. There were no sounds.

They were waiting for what seemed like forever. Then Virginia, feeling brave again, slowly poked her head out of the quilts and over the backboard of their wagon. She couldn't see them. Frantically, she turned her head both ways. They weren't there. She couldn't stand it. She jumped out of the wagon as quietly as she could and said in a low voice, "You stay here. Patty, you know what to do if I scream."

Patty clutched Tommy covering his ears. Her eyes widened and nodded mutely.

With a glance back at them making sure they were covered Virginia made her way stealthily around their wagon. She saw Elitha standing behind her wagon totally hidden but listening to the group which now appeared in front of Elitha's wagon. Virginia crept up to the wagon and hissed, "What is going on?"

Elitha started and grabbed at her heart. "Goodness," she hissed. "You gave me a scare." She took a deep breath. "We are going to trade. These Indians are going to escort us across the prairie and we are going to give them some of our calico prints and tobacco, which they keep calling tabacky." She giggled. "And they will also get some pork and beans and flour."

"Oh," breathed Virginia.

"Your Pa and my pa are saying they can have all of the supplies they are asking for, but not until we safely cross the prairie." Virginia nodded at what she was hearing and was amazed at these Indians. They seemed so different from the ones that their grandmother had told them about in her stories. She thought about her aunt being kidnapped. She looked back at these Indians. They were talking and gesturing to other members in the wagon train. They were so different than she had expected. They didn't look like savages. They were actually communicating with their fathers. No one looked frightened or mad. She thought about her grandmother. She had lived through very different confrontations with Indians. She had warned them to be careful and now, for heaven's sake, they were going to trade with these braves.

Thinking about her grandmother, Virginia began to wonder about her health. These days, she didn't talk so much. Patty had told her she was so worried because Grandmother wouldn't eat. She said she was always trying to tempt her with small bites of biscuits, butter, and honey. She would dip the biscuits in cream to soften the morsels. Usually, they would skim the cream for butter, but Patty wouldn't hear of it. "We have plenty of butter for now and Grandmother Keyes needs this." Of course, the family agreed with her. Virginia remembered seeing her mother cast a worried eye at her mother. She seemed weaker, but she still smiled when Virginia came close to her bed. Movement jarred Virginia out of her reverie.

The men were mounting their horses again and the noise jolted Virginia back to the present. She turned back to go tell Grandmother Keyes about the Indians and then remembered Patty and the boys. She hurried her pace to get back to the wagon to tell them the news. Three heads popped up as Virginia reached the hiding place. She exclaimed that they were trading with these Indians and there was no need to fear them.

The Indians escorted the wagon train across the prairie. The Indians rode along the side of the wagons, and all the children stayed inside the wagons for this part of the trip. They watched with wary eyes as the Indians rode close to their wagons. Virginia kept a rifle under the quilt just in case. She pulled out a mirror and made a show of looking into it and fixing her hair. As one Indian rode up, she showed him the mirror and he got very excited and kept coming back to look at it and then brought two other young Indian boys to come and see this miraculous object.

That night, a spring storm caught them as they were getting ready for the evening. The lightning danced across the sky and loud cracks of thunder kept them awake. The landscape was flat, and they could see for miles. The light show in the sky was fascinating to watch, if not scary, when the thunder seemed to crash right above them and shake their bones. The adults were worried about the huge, rough-toothed spears of lightning finding one of their wagons as an end point to their jagged thrusts. Even though the heavy canvas on the wagons was wet, the fear of fire was terrifying. A fire would burn out a wagon and it would be a disaster. They would lose all their goods and mode of transportation. It would be a long walk to the west coast. For a while, Jimmy felt himself duck every time a boom shook the ground and the wagon, but he got used to it and was even able to sleep after a while. He was unaware that his parents were awake watching the lightning dance across the sky over the darkened waves of the prairie grass below it.

The next morning, the skies were clear. Some areas of prairie grass were laid flat heavy from the rains. Soon, the stalks would be standing tall and waving.

After the incident with the Indians at Soldier Creek, some wagons that had joined the chain decided to break off from the larger train.

"You are moving too slowly. These wagons are too heavy and too large," said one of the men from Jackson, Missouri. He was looking at the "Palace Car" as he was talking. "Our wagons are smaller and we can move quicker. We won't be as large a target for the Indians. We are sorry, but we must move along." With that the smaller wagons continued on ahead at a faster pace.

Virginia, Elitha, and Patty watched the wagons get smaller and smaller as they pulled away from the larger group.

"We'll see them soon enough in Sutter's Fort," Virginia reckoned and wondered if they would ever see them again.

CHAPTER FOUR

The Big Blue - May 26, 1846.

A huge expanse of water stretched before them. The Indians had ridden off and quickly disappeared. They seemed very happy with their payment for escorting the wagon train to the edge of the river.

The gifts to the Indians made little dent into the supplies that the wagons were carrying. Tamsen had enlisted the girls to go through and make an inventory of their caches. They made notes on what bags were opened, half full, or still sealed. There were bags of seeds for planting that had not yet been opened. Surprisingly, the Indians hadn't wanted the seed. The stores of material, the printed cottons, and brightly colored flannels so carefully chosen for trade with the Indians were itemized and the bolts of cloth that had been traded were recorded. They also re-checked the beads, chains, brass finger rings which they had been told would be good for peace offerings to the Indians. There were also yards of lace, muslin, silk for trade. Also, there were satin and velvet for barter with the Mexicans in exchange for land grants in the California Territory. The girls made notations of what supplies were diminishing, what was left and gave the lists to Tamsen.

"Thank you girls," Tamsen had said as they scampered off. She fingered a lovely, large quilt. Not only had she made the quilt especially for the journey, but she had stitched $10,000.00 into the quilt. It was their "just in case" money. The money would remain hidden but close by, and a quilt would always be a very useful item.

Under the Shade of a Huge Oak Tree - May 29, 1846.

Sarah Keyes, mother to Margaret, grandmother to Patty, Virginia,

Tommy, and Jimmy, died peacefully in her sleep. It had not been a surprise. She was getting weaker and weaker and had stopped eating food. The day before she died, she stopped speaking and was breathing so softly and quietly that Patty found she had to rest her hand on her grandmother's chest to make sure she was still alive. She would never see her son Caddan who had gone on to Oregon two years before.

Patty was so sad but also felt that her grandmother would rest peacefully now. The jostling of the wagon on her frail bones had to have been uncomfortable. She watched her mother and father.

"The doctors said she wouldn't have long to live, I just wish she could have lived to reach Fort Hall and see my brother," sniffed Margaret, wiping a tear away from her cheek.

"I'm so sorry, Maggie." He looked into her eyes. "But, she was with *you* and that was most important to her. God allowed her these extra weeks with you." James put his arms around his wife and hugged her close.

Patty stood with tears running down her cheeks. Virginia hugged Patty. "She was our very best grandmother," the girls agreed and each kissed their grandmother's cold cheek.

Patty knelt next to her grandmother. Smoothing the hair her grandmother would never brush again, she pulled out a pair of scissors from her pocket. Cutting a lock of silver grey hair, she kissed it and tied it with ribbon. "I will always carry you with me, Grandmother," she promised and tucked the strand tied with ribbon into her bodice.

The funeral was planned for 2 that afternoon. A cottonwood coffin was made and provided a nice resting place for Grandmother Keyes.

They found a stately White Oak tree, also known as the Monarch Oak, not too far off of the trail. The Reverend Mr. Cornwall prayed and led their goodbye sermon. John Denton, the Englishman traveling with the Donners, carved the headstone that would mark her grave.

"We shall come back to visit you, Grandmother," Patty promised. They lingered a short time longer and then the wagons started down the trail. Patty looked back at the majestic oak tree, the huge branches that reached out providing a large shady area, and she tried to burn that image in her mind so she could easily find it again on her return trip. She tucked her hands under her arms and said one last farewell to her dear grandmother. She felt comforted knowing her grandmother was resting in a lovely, shaded overlook of the trail they were on.

Then they took their leave. Now they were bound for Pawnee territory. Being in Indian Territory, they felt an added excitement and fear.

Eliza and Bayliss were feeling poorly. Some of the other wagons had people who were experiencing the symptoms of diarrhea. It did not help that they had passed several crosses indicating that others had died along the trail. The crosses bore the names and ages of the unfortunate pioneers who would never make it to their destination. Some had died of injuries, while others of diseases as they made their way out west. Those with severe abdominal cramps wondered if they would soon be adding their name to a cross on the lonesome prairie. On the trail, there were no doctors nearby. For one wagon to stop because someone was feeling poorly was not possible. Those who were sick would walk if they could manage, or lie in the wagons groaning, using the wooden bucket, and hoping they would stop soon.

Virginia, Patty, Leanna, and Elitha walked behind the wagons. They were staying more alert looking for any movement off in the distance. The Pawnee were excellent horse riders. Trappers and traders who had visited their campfires at night had told them that the Pawnee liked to trade for foodstuffs. Therefore, they had bags of hog meat, tobacco, and sugar ready for trade.

They had enjoyed their lunch and tea stop and getting out and walking helped with digesting the rich foods they were enjoying. They knew others were sick, but they were enjoying the prairie. The walking was quite easy.

"Eliza thinks that Daisy is off her feed and maybe she has passed something on in her milk," Patty contributed.

"I hope not. I would hate to have to throw out milk, or the cream and butter, she gave this morning." Elitha patted Leanne's hand. "Your head hurt last night, didn't it?"

Leanna nodded, but it felt better today. It was not as if she had the diarrhea.

"I think Aunt Tamsen knows or has an idea of what the cause and possible cure might be. She knows so much about the plants here and what we can eat and what we can make tea from," Patty said. "Maybe Eliza made tea from the wrong root or leaves."

"Well, I hope you're right, because I like the butter and milk we get from Daisy. I don't want to throw it out," declared Virginia. The girls nodded to each other, agreeing that it would be a terrible thing to waste the milk. Having fresh milk, butter, cream, and cheese was a treat they were expecting daily.

Virginia laughed and put her hands on her waist. "I declare, I have gotten fleshier! My dresses are quite tight."

Elitha giggled. "Me, too. In fact, I am not wearing my petticoats and under- garments because they make the bodice too thick and I can't fasten the buttons."

Leanna joined in. "See," she said pulling back on her pinafore, "I don't even fasten the back buttons because they are too tight."

Patty clapped her hands and cried, "Me too!" Indeed, the food had been wondrous. They ate three full meals a day and had afternoon tea with biscuits, butter, jam, sweet cakes, and sometimes sandwiches. There was fresh buffalo meat, berries, wild onions, cream, butter, fresh bread, biscuits, and pies. Eliza made tarts and maple sweets for the children. The food was indeed delicious. Everyone was enjoying the richness and abundance of it.

The girls chatted and giggled as they walked. The sun was slowly setting. They would be stopping soon. The girls split up and checked in with their mothers to be told what the evening duties would be. With Eliza feeling poorly, Virginia and Patty had been helping with the preparation and cooking of the meals.

But tonight, Eliza was feeling fine; she had slept well in the comfort of the wagon. She stuck her head out and caught sight of the girls. "Virginia, go get me some of that sage, the one with silver leaves. I want to put some in the bread for dinner tonight."

Both girls looked at each other and grinned. Oh, good! She was feeling better.

"Yes'm," shouted Virginia and all four girls fanned out towards the sagebrush surrounding the trail. "Mmmm, fresh sagebrush bread and butter. I'll bet she'll put some sage in the prairie chickens Pa caught this afternoon."

"Roasted chicken, fresh bread, sage stuffing, and maybe she'll open a tin of those baby peas." Patty was smiling.

Elitha turned to Virginia and requested, "I sure would like some of that bread."

"I am sure she'll make an extra loaf for you. Aunt Tamsen gave her that tonic and she sure is feeling better now. I am sure she'll want to say thank you."

The girls laughed as they gathered the sage. The pungent scent flavored the air as the soft pale silver-green leaves bruised and gave off their scent. "I'll collect some for Mother," Elitha said, "she likes to perfume the water for soaking our feet as well as adding it to her cooking."

The girls drifted off to begin their evening chores. There was much to set up and get ready for the campfire that evening. Each wagon had their own campfires for dinner, and then everyone got together around one large fire to chat, drink coffee or tea, and entertain themselves with stories, songs, and dancing.

The men checked the wagons, as they did every evening. There was always a thorough inspection of all livestock and equipment. The huge wagon wheels were checked for dents, gouges, or signs of wearing or weakening metal. They unhitched the oxen and set them up with water and hay. The oxen and cattle were given cursory exams to check their hooves for rocks, splits, or redness. Milt and the other drivers checked the leather reins and each bridle for wear and nicks. Large hands felt along the smooth wooden surfaces of oxen harnesses to inspect for cracks, nicks, or wearing edges. The horses needed brushing, their hooves checked for splinters, uneven wearing, or breaks. Then the hooves were oiled and the horses watered and fed. Virginia much preferred helping brush, water, and feed the horses than working to prepare, cook, and clean up after meals. Eliza had Patty to help her, so Virginia usually went to help her father with the horses. They were always careful to hobble the horses in the evening so they would not wander off. There was nothing worse than getting up in the morning to find your horse had wandered off because you had forgotten to tether the ties or secure their legs. They could be a mile away or further, and the time lost looking or worse, the loss of a horse to a predator or injury was a terrible price for stupidity.

That evening, as they gathered again around one large campfire, stories were told, songs were sung, and everyone felt the cohesiveness of the group. To a chorus of "goodnights," the group went to bed to a warm, comfortable sleep.

In the morning, after a good, hearty breakfast, the wagons were hitched up to the huge oxen and the morning trail began. What a joyous time for the children. Walking behind the wagons, riding inside or on horseback, they had time to play, talk, and sing. Tommy was looking for a coyote pup to catch and tame. They all talked excitedly about no school, no school books, no testing. Virginia was especially glad because she found reading boring and writing tiresome. Although she did promise to keep a journal, she did not want to, but felt that with Patty's help, she could probably do so. So she began one dutifully filling the pages as the trip progressed.

Eliza was secretly glad that Aunt Tamsen had brought along books and chalk slates. She missed school and did enjoy reading and writing. Her penmanship was beautiful. She practiced her ABCs and writing when Virginia was composing in her journal.

As they walked along following the wagon train, the children kept an eye out for wildlife. There were prairie dogs, which they enjoyed watching, laughing at the squeaks and antics and the way they stood on their hind legs. There were antelope herds, of which savory roasts were made. The buffalo could be seen off in the distance, which promised fresh meat when the men went out to hunt them. But more distressing and ever-present were buffalo flies. Huge black flies with the ability to cause considerable welts when they bit were so aggravating. The bites would sting, itch, and irritate often leading to large, red, hard, infected bumps and skin rashes.

Often, Indians would come and ride along the wagon train or follow at a distance. The Minneconjou bucks or boys would ride close, whoop, and show off their horsemanship. Hanging off the back of the Palace wagon was a mirror, and the boys liked to ride up, catch their reflection, whoop, and ride off. Those in the long line of trains were beginning to tell the difference between the various tribes of Indians. As they passed through territories, they saw earthen lodges, in which the Pawnee lived. They saw tents and teepees and wooden lean-to structures. They were seeing more Indians representing different tribes. Who knew there were so many different kinds of Indians and Indian languages? They looked differently too. They learned which Indians were friendly, and which bore a watchful eye.

Virginia and Elitha especially kept an eye on the Indians. As they progressed across the prairie grass, they saw Sioux Indians riding their horses at a far distance. The Sioux had a fierce reputation among other Indians and the Whites. They could turn and attack or wait until nightfall and raid the sleeping pioneers stealing animals, killing those who fought, and kidnapping others (either Indians from other tribes or the Whites) for slaves. The Sioux were brutal and whenever they were around, the whole wagon train was on alert. Rifles were kept loaded and within reach inside the wagons as well as knives or hand guns at the ready for those on horseback. They rode on silently, and suddenly, the Sioux following them along the ridge disappeared. They remained vigilant because they could and would be back. They passed Indian lodges where more herds of buffalo and dogs tagging along behind their Indian masters were seen. The Sioux were a threat to other Indians as well, so they had a common foe, and Virginia was sorry when they pulled away from the Indian villages and the train was on its own again.

That evening, after dinner and then gathering around the giant campfire, the group was subdued. It seemed like a longer day because they had to be so vigilant and keep a watch out for the Sioux. Soon the songs started and as people sang, the atmosphere of worry lessened. A favorite song of Patty's was "Mr. Froggy went a Courtin'." She sang loudly and clapped when it was over. Other folk songs accompanied the singing with rousing notes from accordions and harmonicas. The evening was cool and pleasant. The bug population decreased as the night became cooler and they listened to the frogs and crickets singing in the background. Things were so comfortable, sitting or lying on the grass, the fire light dancing off the smiling faces as they sang or played an instrument. Cash propped his head on Patty's lap and nudged her hand with his nose. She petted the silky brown head–pure contentment. Now that the fears from the day had passed, they had eaten, bedded down the livestock, prepared for tomorrow, and the rest of the evening was theirs to sing, dance, tell stories, and then be off to sleep.

It was not unusual for other travelers on the trail to join their campfires in the evenings. Many of those who asked to partake in that evening's entertainment were the trappers and hunters who traveled through the territories. Although these men were tough and mostly traveled on horseback with few of the conveniences that they had in their wagon train, these men were friendly and great providers of information. They would tell them about the trails ahead and how many wagon trains they had seen and how large each one was. They told about the weather, trail conditions, and problem Indian areas. They would also offer to carry back letters and journal articles to be posted for mail in the first large city they reached. Some of the travelers posted articles to be printed in newspapers or in journals so others could decide if a trip out west was for them. Tamsen always had letters to go back home to Springfield to let family and friends know what life on the trail was like. These services the men brought to wagon trains were traded for a hot home cooked dinner, breakfast, warm water and soap, and maybe some bread or biscuits for the next day. They hit the "mother lode" with Eliza's biscuits, cobbler, jams, and fresh butter. Many men would shake their head in amazement to see the sweet-faced, brown-eyed cow chewing her cud hitched to the back of the huge two-storied wagon. They had to admit, since the daily pace was slow, the cow had no trouble keeping up and she contributed wonders to the diet.

Edwin Bryant, a newspaperman, was a short-time member of the wagon train. He often sent back articles for publication with the trappers. The newspapers often printed his articles of life on the trail. Although not a member of the Donner-Reed wagon train, he voiced his concerns of their slow progress and often complained when the wagon train took long days of rest. He felt that getting to Fort Laramie at the end of June was very late in the summer.

"I have told you, all the other travelers have moved along the trail so much more quickly. It is almost June. Bad weather and an early snowfall could cause some terrible troubles for this train," he would warn.

"Yes, yes," comforted George Donner, "but we are moving along fine. We need these stops and the weather and the trail will hold."

Patty watched Tamsen shake her head. "Maybe we should increase our pace, George," Tamsen said.

"Now, now, Tamsen, Mr. Bryant is a high falootin' newspaper man. Everything is done at top speed. We are doing fine."

Tamsen wanted to say more, but James rode up on his horse to talk with George and the newspaper man, and she knew to hold her own counsel.

Mr. Bryant shook his head as he rode away from the men. They would only have these short summer months in which to travel the rest of the distance. He knew the trail became more difficult and the weather would become an increasing problem. He tried to talk with the other men in the wagon train trying to urge their forward progress at a faster speed, but to no avail. They were happy with their progress. The trail was easy, the food good and bountiful, so if they arrived a bit later into the fall, they would be fine. After many tries and urging the group to move more quickly, he decided to continue on alone at a faster speed. He left the wagon train the next morning.

CHAPTER FIVE

The Disastrous Reading of the Hastings Doctrine - Fort Laramie, June, 1846

Fort Laramie turned out to be a bustling community. Fort Laramie was originally developed by fur traders in 1834. It was at the confluence of the North Platte and Laramie rivers. {As it became a bustling entity, the U.S Military purchased it in 1849 and they named it in honor of the fur trader, Jacques Le Ramie.}

On approach, Virginia, George, Elitha, and Patty spied teepees. There was a long line of teepees in front of the fort and behind it. It seemed like a whole village of Indians lived on the outside of the fort. Outside their teepees were blankets and furs on round stretchers. As they skinned the animals they caught, the Indians saved the meat and then treated and scraped off the soft underside of the skin and then stretched the fur into usable pieces. These would become muffs, blankets, shirts, skirts, and hats.

They passed more groups of Indians with their dogs as they came closer to the fort. Anticipation mounted as they passed so closely to these wild savages, and surprisingly, the Indians paid them no mind. It seemed like a huge Indian village was accepted and lived outside the fort walls. The daily life of children, dogs, eating and sleeping, hunting and cooking happened casually on the slopes leading to the fort. As the wagon train pulled up to the fort walls, the pioneer children smiled and laughed with excitement. They marveled and wondered what life would be like and how it would be for them joining such a huge fort.

There were men with guns propped beside them positioned along the top and at the corners of the fort walls. The fort entrance, which was open, was a huge double door that swung inward. People, horses, donkeys, and wagons seemed to be in constant flow in and out of the fort.

George, Mary, Elitha, and Leanna went exploring. After promising not to get in anyone's way, they took off. They ran along the rough-hewn boards and boldly peeked in rooms whose doors were open. Many rooms had bedsteads, some with blankets, some without. There were Indians and Cowboys sitting and talking and smoking in the middle of several rooms. Buffalo hides were providing a place for them to sit. They gathered around in one room and used a small table in the center as the surface to cut their tobacco.

Patty and Virginia left shortly after the first group, cautiously peeking into rooms looking for their friends.

"What are you doing?" asked Virginia who had been searching for them and finally caught up to them.

"Come and watch," urged George, motioning Virginia to join them. They watched the men cutting tobacco, shuffling cards, and talking.

Patty was getting bored. "Let's go see what else we can find." The group took off down the hallway.

The group split in half as Virginia, Eddie, and George decided to go look at the stables, while the girls wanted to explore the general store and the store's hold.

The general store was full from floor to ceiling with shelves that stretched the length of the room.

"Just like the mercantile!" Patty breathed. "Only better and so much more."

There were blankets, furs, bolts of cloth, pots and pans, and shelves with nothing but canned goods on them. There were nails, strips of leather, kerosene cans, wax and candles, soap, shoe leather, rope, and a whole section of liniments, elixirs, pills, and other health nostrums.

"Yes, so much better," Leanne agreed. She stroked the beaver pelt that was stretched on a large round hoop placing each leg of the beaver and its tail so they attached to the sides of the hoop. There were also wolf, coyote, rabbit, weasel, beaver, buffalo, deer, fox, and cowhides piled from the floor. Other furs stretched on hoops and lined up were leaning against the wall. Indian trade blankets of red, green, and yellow stripes were piled in great heaps on the floor.

"My goodness, have you ever seen so many lovely things in one room?" Mary exclaimed. "This room is bigger than a stable." She looked around and then spied the candy on the shelf by the cash box.

The girls gathered around to look at the brightly colored sweets. Penny candy in all colors and flavors sparkled by the candle that had been set on the counter. They didn't have any money.

"Let's go get some pennies from Pa," suggested Patty. With that, the group ran out to reunite with the wagon train and get some spending pennies.

Virginia, George, and Eddie came back from exploring the stables and stopped by a large room. Inside were many men from their wagon train.

"I'm just saying beware of the golden shores you seek," a man was warning.. He was Jim Clyman. He had been to the west and had come back. "There is sparse rain and ruined crops. I have been the way of Hastings' new route. We went to the Humboldt by Fort Bridger. The salt desert and the Great Salt Lake are treacherous at best. There is no water and I found no clear-cut path. You would be better off to take the established trail if you wish to get there. It is not as he claims."

"This shortcut of Hastings will save us time. It will cut off at least two weeks of travel." Virginia looked up to see her father talking. He was answering the man called Jim Clyman who wore very tattered and dirty leggings and a long buckskin coat with several worn areas. He had grey long hair and a grey beard.

The man with the long grey beard snorted and coughed into his hand. "You think you know what is ahead? I do. Who are you going to listen to?" he challenged the men sitting around the tables and on the floor.

"Yeah, you tell 'em, Jim!" A grizzled man with dirty ginger hair to his shoulders encouraged. He drank his beer spilling it down his front.

"We really think a man who has written a book about the way to go has some knowledge," James snidely quipped.

"Yes," agreed George.

"I am saying it isn't so." Mr. Clyman folded his arms across his chest, his lips pressed into a thin line. "The route by Fort Hall is hard enough to travel, and if you leave that route, it becomes impossible to pass, even on horseback. I can't imagine trying to get through with a wagon. No sir, you best take the Oregon trail way."

"Yeah," chorused several of the on-lookers.

"You city-folk like to take the easy way, and there ain't no easy way," the old explorer hit the table in frustration. His beer slopped as he angrily picked it up.

"Thank you for your information, sir." Mr. Reed stiffened at the sound of his fist hitting the table. He turned his back on the negative Mr. Clyman. "Mr. Hastings has written a book. He can show us the way. Three hundred and fifty miles is a long way to cut off. There isn't any reason for us to not take the short cut."

"Have it your way, Mr." Mr. Clyman got up abruptly and finished, "I can't help but think this is the wrong decision and you will be sorry."

The men fell to discussing the pros and cons, gathering around the rough-hewn table. A few women, Tamsen included, stood on the periphery and listened to the talk.

Jacob Donner agreed with the talk of taking the short cut. "I have the book," he said, holding up the thin blue book and showing the group. "*At the headlands of the Sweetwater. To all California Emigrants now on the road,*" Lansford Hastings urged them to take the short cut. "It will save 350 miles," and he added, "Mr. Hastings says that large groups are a good defense against those who don't want us there." He pantomimed pulling an arrow out of his quiver and shooting it. "This is the way to go."

Later, back in his wagon, Jacob was explaining the rationale of taking the little-known Hastings route.

"I agree with both James Reed and Jacob," said George Donner. He watched his wife straighten up and prepare their wagon for an early start the next morning.

Tamsen shook out a tablecloth and shook her head at the same time. She was concerned about this talk of a short cut. No one knew this Lansford Hastings; they only knew him by what others were saying and what his book claimed. She doubted that this would be a great time saver. There had been no one who had yet reported on the success of this short cut. She shivered. There was something about this new plan she didn't like. She had heard the talk from many other travelers and those who had not taken the Oregon Trail had many stories of hardships. She and George had discussed the short cut at length, but he was adamant.

"I do not believe this is the way for us to go," she insisted. "I believe what Jim Clyman said. He said the wagons could not pass through this trail."

George laughed. "He is a very old man and only rides his horse. Lansford Hastings wrote a book and he has traveled all over the Oregon and California Territories. We men discussed our options and we will be leaving early tomorrow and take the Hastings cut off."

Tamsen heard his words, but she was not convinced. It didn't matter because the majority of the wagon train had voted for the short cut. She believed that this might lengthen their trip. It was the end of June already.

There was another problem pressuring the group. It was very late in the year to be traveling west. The emigrants were among the last group to be leaving Fort Laramie. If they could save two hundred miles at a minimum and up to 350 miles, then the short cut made sense. The other positive was that Hastings said he would wait for the wagon train at Fort Bridger and personally take them through the short cut. How could they go wrong? They were saving hundreds of miles and would have a guide. Both James Reed and George Donner felt that the Left Hand Turn short cut would be the best route.

They left the next morning. Then, after the Fourth of July, one more family arrived at Fort Laramie. They found themselves making a late start to the California territory. Because they wanted to join another group for company and protection, they decided to also take the Left Hand Turn and took off after the Donner party. They were the Graves family who numbered thirteen in adults and children. They also agreed to take the Hastings cut-off so they could catch up with the Reed-Donner party that had left the week earlier.

*   *   *   *   *

June 29, 1846

The Donner Wagon Train started very early the next morning. It was before sunrise. The time had come to say goodbye to the friends they had made at Fort Laramie. Tamsen was feeling gloomy and she couldn't shake the heavy sense of foreboding this new Left Hand Turn short cut was sure to bring. "I fear we are making a grave mistake," she said to herself, "for us to leave the old route to try a new one we know nothing about and to attempt it without anyone here to help us find our way. I am so afraid." She bent down and half-heartedly swept the floor. As she turned to leave, she smoothed the quilt that covered their bed. Fingering the stiff border of the quilt, she felt somewhat comforted that they did have the funds to help them through the worst of times. She then straightened her shoulders, smoothed her apron over her skirt, and set about her chores.

She then collected her girls. "Tomorrow, I would like you to keep an eye out for some Prairie Turnips or Indian Turnips as they are also called. They will be easy to spot because they grow high."

"How high should we be looking?" asked Elvina.

"At least a foot high." Mrs. Donner held her hand out palm downward showing how high a foot would be. "You'll see from the base many spike-like branches and small clusters of blue flowers. If you pull them, there will be 3 or 4 tubers which I can then peel."

"What shall you make of them?" inquired Elitha.

"They shall make a fine additional vegetable to our supper tonight."

The girls collected baskets and made ready for the day's journey. They were successful in finding several of the turnips and when they were roasted that evening, they were delicious.

The Breens Make the Right Decision - July 11, 1846

The next morning, it took a very long time to get everyone moving. Maybe that was fortuitous because otherwise they may not have received the warning.

As they broke camp late, it was 11:00 am, and they were still preparing to leave when a messenger rode into camp. The Pawnees had murdered a Mr. Trimble. They were to find out later that he was a member of the Graves group before they joined the Donner party. There was rumor that a band of Sioux was due at their camp that afternoon.

With fear and trepidation, they broke camp quickly and took off into the Black Hills, later called the Laramie Hills.

Mr. Breen commented to his wife, "We are so fortunate to have caught up with this final wagon-train. I would not have wanted to be out on the prairie with no protection against the Sioux."

The Meeting at Independence Rock - July 12, 1846

The Breen family with Patrick Dolan and the Graves all joined the Donner party at Independence Rock. The huge, grey granite rock loomed before the travelers and they could see it for miles out. The rock was a kind of information center with travelers leaving their names as proof they were there. The group set about inscribing their names, that day's date or their birth dates. After chiseling their messages in the communication rock, they set about to welcome the newcomers. The Breens were an Irish family and devoted Catholics; Patrick was the father and Peggy the wife the same age as her husband. They had seven children: John, the eldest, then Eddie, Patrick, Simon, Peter, James, and Isabella, one-year-old and the only girl.

The evenings were so much more fun since Patrick Dolan had joined them. In the evening, one of the wagons would drop its back wall providing a dance surface for the Irishman. Then to lively music, he would dance the Irish jig and teach the others how to do it too. There would be clapping and singing and every young woman and girl learned to dance.

The Donner party wagon train had indeed grown. As more and more families found they were going in the same direction, they felt they should join each other. As they left Independence, the wagon train had between two and three hundred wagons. The long chain of white covered wagons, teams of oxen, horses, walking children, dogs, and adults stretched for over two miles. By now, they had voted on the leader for the wagon train. Although James Reed was younger, stronger, a good provider, and a good leader, many people preferred the soft, good-natured George Donner. In the end, George was elected to be leader of their wagon train and thus it became to be known as the Donner Wagon train or the Donner party.

One afternoon as they were rumbling along, James Reed spotted buffalo out in the distance. "I'm going after some fresh meat," he promised Margaret. He took off at a gallop. Margaret smiled as he disappeared. It would be good to have more fresh meat, and she wanted to have another skin to use as a blanket.

That evening, as they were releasing the oxen to graze and making the evening fires, James rode in driving a buffalo. He had slightly wounded the shoulder of the beast and he was behind the buffalo moving him towards the camp. "This way, there will be no loss of meat. Everyone can cut off steaks and pack the extra meat for travel. The fat can be collected and you have yourself a fine skin, Margaret."

That night, the entertainment seemed merrier. Their diet was fortified with plentiful antelope and buffalo steaks. Being well-fed put everyone in a festive mood and the dancing and the singing grew louder.

July 18, the Continental Divide

The continental divide runs from northwestern Canada along the crest of the Rocky Mountains to New Mexico. Then it follows the crest of Mexico's Sierra Madre Occidental. The Great Divide is not so much a physical landmark as it is a geographical marker. At this point in the United States, rain or snow that drains on the east side of the Continental Divide flows toward the Atlantic Ocean, while precipitation on the west side drains and flows toward the Pacific Ocean. It is an unusual phenomenon. At that location, all rivers would be running towards the Great Divide. Also from the top of the Divide, they could trace out their route from the east side of the Great Salt Lake.

The families, the Breens and the Graves, who had joined them also included Mary Ann Graves, a beautiful young woman who had the single men making excuses to talk with her and finding ways to help her. Mary Ann had seven younger brothers and sisters. Adding that to the Breen family of six boys and one girl increased the population of the Donner party by twenty.

The road had become very difficult for travel. They passed standing pools of poisoned water. Selenium salts had seeped into the ground water, and standing water became contaminated by Purple Locoweed, Milk Vetch, or Prince's Plume. This reaction, also known as Bobtail disease, cause hoofed animals to develop a staggering gate and they wander aimlessly eating any green vegetation whether it is digestible or not. Everyone was cautioned not to let any animal drink the water. There was alkali in the pools and when the cattle and oxen would drink it, they would become ill slowing progress even more. Tamsen appointed herself as the water safety monitor and she continued up and down the wagon train reminding people not to let the oxen drink. The dogs sniffed and then wisely avoided the puddles.

Charles T. Stanton called the Continental Divide the "culminating point," the Rubicon that he had crossed. "Now the rivers flowed to the Pacific," he proclaimed and he would soon reach the end of his journey and get paid for his efforts.

At this time, Edwin Bryant, the newspaperman, was already at Fort Bridger. Remember, he had become irritated with the slow process of the wagon train, so he left and was way ahead of the group. He had decided to take his mule train over the proposed route of Lansford Hastings. He chose this route because mountain man Jim Bridger, of great reputation, recommended this new way as well. He did not know that both Louis Vasquez and Jim Bridger were partners trying to increase travel and commerce through Fort Bridger and therefore were promoting the Lansford Hasting "short cut" even though it was not a proven road. The Bryant mule-train had a very difficult time in making the Hastings passage. They were men on mules with no heavy wagons to bog them down and didn't have to fuss with families or children. Still, the route was near impossible. This fact, and more, made Edwin Bryant write to his friend Jim Reed a letter telling them NOT to go that way. While still on the impassable trail, he sent the letter back to Mr. Vasquez and Mr. Bridger to deliver to the Reeds when their wagon train arrived at Fort Bridger. Louis Vasquez kept the letter in his pocket and did not deliver it as Mr. Bryant had wanted. So the final warning that may have made a difference to the Donner party was not delivered.

July 19, the Little Sandy. Sweetwater County, Wyoming

The Little Sandy River became a favorite campsite for travelers going west. Depending upon the year's rainfall, the water would be welcome. Although during drought, the river would be dry, sandy, and caked with clay, sage brush, and thistles.

As the wagon train approached the Little Sandy, the lead wagon driven by George Donner spotted a willow and canvas enclosure. He saw something move—a figure.

"Whoa!" he shouted to the oxen and jumped off of the buckboard. "Hello," he called into the mound of tree saplings and canvas. A pale head poked out.

"Please, stop," a feeble voice was barely heard speaking.

"Who are you, son, and what are you doing here?" asked the concerned Captain.

"My name, Sir, is Luke Halloran. I was riding on horseback with a group but have become so ill I can't stay on my mount. They left me here in hopes that a kind wagon Captain would pick me up and let me ride in their wagon." He looked up expectantly.

George had his doubts about adding another person to their wagon train. He felt that they had already taken in extra people and he had no room in his already crowded wagons. He shook his head no, turned around, got back up on his wagon, and was about to urge the beasts to pull their burden when he heard and felt a flurry of skirts on his left.

Tamsen, drawing herself up to her full five-foot height, told George she thought they did indeed have room for one more. Hands on her hips and her mouth set just so, she had drawn herself up to her full height and George knew when he was licked. He looked down at the poor, bedraggled boy. He sighed and acquiesced.

Tamsen assured him she could nurse Luke and with the abundance of food and the easy trail road, it wouldn't be much of an imposition.

George smiled fondly at his wife. Of course she would want to care for this young man. He helped him into their wagon and shouted "g'up," to his oxen.

Tamsen was glad that George had changed his mind and allowed the poor boy to join them. She knew her husband's kind heart would win out. That poor Luke was looking and feeling poorly. He was unable to ride his horse and the jolting of the wagon made travel difficult enough for him. She was certain if the boy were left by the roadside, he would surely die. She wasn't sure about his chances with them but knew they were better than to be discarded by the roadway.

As they were deciding the fate of Luke Halloran, the body of the wagon train was gathering to decide who was going to split off. Several wagons decided to take the longer, more established Sublette route to Oregon and California. The remainder of the Donner party continued on to Fort Bridger and followed the Hastings trail. The next morning, the die was cast.

That evening, around the campfire, the group sat down to discuss who would lead the wagon train.

"I am thinking James Reed should lead us. He has done a good job leading the way and finding food, and he has been with the wagon train since the beginning," Mr. Graves began the conversation.

"No, I'm a thinkin' that's not such a good idea. He can be kinda uppity," replied another. "I like George Donner as our leader."

"Let's take a vote," Mr. Breen said.

With that, George Donner was elected Captain of the Reed-Donner party, what was to become known as the Donner Party.

July 20, the Left Hand Turn, the Hastings Cut Off

{Today is the fateful day that the Reed-Donner wagon train makes the decision to take the Left Hand Turn, the Hastings short cut, that will determine their fates and put the name Donner in the history books.}

The group came to the now infamous fork in the road. To the right, the road went up to Fort Hall and was the proven trail. The road to the left was the one touted by Lansford Hastings as the short cut (and unbeknownst to them, never taken by Mr. Hastings) was the way the group majority voted to follow. They believed the few men who had promised this route as the best way to travel. It was getting later in the summer, already past summer solstice, and the weather would be getting cooler and the days shorter.

{The letter Edwin Bryant wrote and sent back to his friends specifically warning James Reed and the others not to go that way was never delivered and never read.}

Tamsen Donner had spoken out against this short cut and had tried to persuade her husband George not to take it. George believed along with Jim Reed and several of the other men that this was the best strategy for the wagon train. Tamsen wondered why they would follow the word of a man, Lansford Hastings, whom they did not know. Even though he had written a book, she believed the words of Mr. Clyman when he warned them of the dangers of the "short-cut." Ignoring her protestations, the Left Hand Turn was taken.

"Now, now," said George, patting her hand. "You will see. This is a much faster way and we do need to go a bit faster now. So rest easy, my dear, you shall see." He smiled and shouted at the oxen, and their heavy wagon started to roll forward along with the others.

July 21-24, the Dreadful Dry 83 Miles South of the Great Salt Lake

They had traveled maybe twenty miles on the Left Hand Turn. Now traveling towards Fort Bridger, four oxen died from drinking tainted water which lies in stagnant puddles in Dry Sandy Creek. *Great name,* mused Tamsen, rolling with bumps and jostles of the rough ground.

Tamsen found the caring of Luke a way to occupy her time on the rough road. He was quite ill, had a persistent cough, and was very thin and weak. She suspected that he had Tuberculosis, a wasting lung disease that makes breathing more difficult. She hoped that when they reached the sunny climes of California, he would rest better and get stronger.

The possible loss of the oxen was a constant worry and the foul, stagnant, poisonous water did not bode well for the travelers. The oxen were their lifeblood for getting the wagons to their final destination. If they died or were poisoned, the entire traveling party would be doomed.

The Breen family was behind the George Donner wagon. The Breens had three wagons containing the parents and seven children.

Mr. Breen's friend, Patrick Dolan, was in a wagon behind them. Patrick Dolan became a favorite of the children because of his wonderful storytelling about Ireland–the world of fairies, pixies, and banshees who rode on wicked winds in the moonlight. He was also a grand dancer and often in the evening would encourage those sitting by the campfire to sing and dance.

At night, around the campfire, there was grumbling and complaining about the horrid water and loss of oxen. Long gone were the festive evening dances and singing despite the best efforts of Patrick. Jim Reed tried to minimize the unhappiness telling them to think of the time they were saving. George Donner chimed in telling them they would be able to buy fresh oxen at Fort Bridger. Other men joined the conversation, some complaining, some bolstering up the rightness of their move. Others said that maybe the other trail to Fort Hall would be just as difficult as this one. And really, how would they know? In the end, they all agreed that shortening the trip could only work out to be the best for them.

July 28, Fort Bridger

Fort Bridger, established by Jim Bridger and Louis Vasquez in 1842, was not like Fort Laramie. It was very small and there were a few crudely built cabins. There were fewer people visiting the fort; therefore, the hustle and bustle that made Fort Laramie exciting was not there. The fort was founded in 1842, but most provisions and supplies did not arrive until 1843. Thus, it was a relatively new fort. It does lie in a beautiful little valley with a creek which keeps the banks green. As they approached the fort, long before they reached the wooden walls, they saw vast stretches of Indians, teepees, and cook fires. Patty wondered at the numbers of Indians surrounding the fort. It seemed like the whole Indian Nation was there.

In later years, Fort Bridger became an import outpost for emigrant wagon trains, the Pony Express, and the Overland stage stop.

Patty, walking alongside the wagon, gazed in disappointment at the meager encampment. There was a sea of Indian lodgings, but the crude fort fence encompassed a very small working fort. She, as did the other children, was hoping for the great stores and huge gatherings of people. Certainly, there would be penny sweets and interesting articles for sale. But alas, there were so fewer visitors here compared to Fort Laramie. As they looked at what they had for sale, their disappointment increased. The trade tended more to necessary articles of clothing, travel, and cooking. The traders they did see were dressed in buckskins. Shirts, skirts, and moccasins were made of deerskin, and these the traders were eager to trade with the pioneers. They were hoping this new wagon train would have desired articles for trade or sale.

George and James had planned to meet up with other emigrants waiting at the fort for more wagons. They wanted to make a larger train to continue on the purported route that was to cut off 250 miles. There was always safety in numbers.

On this July 28, they arrived at Fort Bridger. To the group's great dismay, they found that Lansford Hastings, the man who was to escort them through the short cut, had already left.

It was said that Hastings' group had waited as long as he had felt was prudent. Then they left.

"What? No escort? How are we going to find our way?" raged Jim Reed. Many of the emigrants were upset. How could this be? How would they be able to maneuver through country that no one was familiar with or even knew the correct way to follow? The men convened as a group and talked about their options. They decided that a four-day rest at Bridger would be in order. They would repair some of the wagon wheels and reinforce wagon walls and conduct other repairs. The delay wouldn't cost them time, they reasoned, because the new trail would be much easier, since they had been told that the new route was more open, and shorter than the Fort Hall road. Jim Bridger told them about the easier trail. He also maintained that although Hastings had gone ahead, there would be no difficulty in catching up with him, or following the trail and the notes he would leave for them. On July 31st, four days later, the Donner-Reed party left Fort Bridger.

Outside Fort Bridger,
Medical Care on the Pioneer Trail

"Come on Eddie, let's go!" Virginia urged her new friend. "Come on, the others have already taken off." With that, Virginia swung up onto Billy and, hair streaming behind her, took off at a gallop.

Eddie Breen yelled, "Wait up!" He mounted his horse and took off after her and the rest of the group. They soon caught up with the group and explored ahead of the wagon train. They were having a wonderful time whooping like Indians themselves, charging each other, and exploring the countryside.

Suddenly, a scream pierced the air. Turning back, Virginia saw Eddie and his horse in mid-tumble. The horse somersaulted headfirst with Eddie following on horseback into the roll, and briefly, the large equine mass covered and then squashed him underneath. He lay on the ground motionless while his horse scrambled to her feet.

"Eddie!" shouted Virginia as she jumped off her horse. "Are you hurt?"

"Oh, my leg!" cried Eddie, trying to sit up. "She fell on my leg and crushed it. Oh, it's broken," he moaned, rocking back and forth.

Virginia gently took off his boot and sock. She rolled up his pant leg. "Oh, I think you're right. It's broken." She looked up as the others rode in to see what was going on.

George Donner, John, and Patrick Breen Jr. dismounted.

"Oh Eddie, it does look broken," lamented John, "I'd better ride back and get Pa." With that, he swung up on his horse and took off back towards the wagon train.

The others stood around the distraught boy lying moaning on the ground. There was nothing to say. A broken leg? This would mean amputation.

Patrick Breen rode on horseback to his son while his anxious wife urged the oxen to quicken their pace moving their heavy wagon so she could be with her son.

As the wagon caught up to where Eddie lay, Peggy Breen could see her son was very pale and hardly moving. She climbed down from the wagon and covered the distance to him quickly. She looked at her husband, he shook his head. Bending down, she gently ran her hand up and down Eddie's leg.

"Oh Eddie. Your leg is broken for sure. We will send back to Fort Bridger for the doctor."

"You can't cut it off!" cried Eddie, "I won't let you!" He knew what the doctor would do.

"There, there, son. It will be what it will be. Let's see what the doctor says," soothed his mother as his father took off riding back to Fort Bridger. "Help me get him into the wagon," asked Peggy to the crowd gathering around them.

They got him into the wagon and tried to make him comfortable. Eddie screamed as they heaved him into the wagon. He cried and screamed whenever he had to move his leg. They cut his pant leg off as the leg became red and swollen, and then started to turn black and blue. Then they waited for the doctor to arrive.

Hours later, when the doctor arrived, Eddie stared at him in horror. He was an old man. His dirty, stringy hair straggled out of his hat. He was unshaven, his vest stiff and dirty with what looked like blood. His hands and nails were dirty and his manner was very gruff. A smell permeated the wagon as he swung up into the bed and peered at the mangled leg.

"Yep, leg's broken and it has to come off," he announced.

"No!" answered Eddie.

"Now Eddie," his mother tried to intervene.

"No, please don't let him cut my leg off. No. No. I will not have it done. I cannot. Please Ma, no!" pleaded Eddie.

"You have to have it cut off. Blood poisoning will set in and you'll die," retorted the doctor. "Now, someone hold him down."

With those words, Eddie became desperate and tried to get up and run away. He kept screaming and crying and his mother was worried he would die right then. He kept crying "no!" repeatedly.

Mrs. Breen did not like the look of the doctor and she sympathized with her son. What good is a boy or man without a leg?

Eddie kept pleading with her to leave his leg alone.

The doctor was becoming more and more impatient. "I rode all the way out here. It is time to cut the leg off so I can get back to the Fort. It is getting near dark." He was worried about meeting Indians in his way. He wasn't about to be killed going home late because some young child was afraid. He glared at Peggy. "What's it going to be?" he asked harshly. He drew a black bundle from his doctor's bag and unwound the material. A dull saw was brandished and the doctor repeated himself, "What's it going to be, boy?"

Eddie was inconsolable. He would not cut off his leg. He would rather die.

"Well, boy, that's what you are going to do, die."

With that, the odious doctor wiped his hands together. "Well then, are you going to let that boy decide?" he asked Mrs. Breen, incredulous that she was listening to this wet-behind-the-ears cub. He looked to her husband for someone with some sense…

Now, Patrick Breen was a practical man, but he loved his children. He felt Eddie was old enough to make that decision. He also knew if the pain and blood poisoning did start, he could amputate the leg. God willing, he would do a just job. He felt he was as qualified and more sanitary than the doctor was. He looked at his wife and nodded.

She looked at her piteous son and again at the nasty-natured doctor. "I am going to let him decide," she said determinedly.

Shaking his head, he slapped his hat on his head and swung out of the wagon leaving his stench behind him. They could hear him muttering. He untied his horse and swung up. Mrs. Breen pressed some money into his hand and thanked him for coming out.

"It's his funeral," he snapped and spurred his mule.

Mrs. Breen turned back to the wagon. Eddie was rocking back and forth crying, but more quietly to himself. "Well, let's make you more comfortable, Eddie. We need to get this wagon moving on."

His friends waved good-bye as they turned forward to the beginning of the wagon train. Patty came alongside the wagon and gave Eddie a warm quilt to help cushion his leg. Tamsen sent a tea of healing herbs instructing Peggy to give it to Eddie every few hours. "It will help him sleep and will take the edge off of his pain," she said. She squeezed Peggy's arm in support and smiled and walked away to her wagon. She waved as the larger train got restarted.

The Breens watched the others leave. Peggy set to brewing some tea. When everything was in order, she nodded to her husband and he snapped the oxen to begin moving forward. Straining against the wooden yokes and the leather harnesses, the beasts slowly pulled the wagon gaining speed and plodded forward to join the rest of the wagon train, which they could see in the distance. Brave little Eddie gritted his teeth and with each jarring roll of the wagon, they began their progress forward.

August 1, 1846

Mary Murphy awoke early the next morning. She lay there thinking. She was anxious to get to know more of the people on the wagon train. Her mother had decided to take the family out west; now that their father had died, she was willing to take the family out west for better opportunities. The children had all agreed to help. Mary was only 14, but she had many chores which she had assumed as the oldest daughter. Her brother John was 16 now and considered one of the men really. He worked the teams and helped their sister Sarah's husband William Foster deal with the endless repairs on the wagons, on the tack, and everything else that seemed to go wrong on the trail.

Mary had hung back and watched the scene unfold with little Eddie the day before. She wondered how he was doing and if he would lose his leg to the crush injury. She was glad they didn't have to amputate his leg like the doctor had wanted to. She admired Eddie's courage and hoped that keeping his leg would not be a death sentence for him. Out here on the trail, away from any good doctors or medicine, the travelers knew illness or injury could mean death.

She quickly slipped out from under the quilt. The nights were still warm and a covering was only needed in the early morning when the air was cool, and sometimes there was dampness in the morning air when they camped near the water. Being careful not to wake anyone in the wagon, she took a bucket, climbed out of the wagon, and went to the water to fill it. Bringing the heavy, sloshing bucket back, she placed it on the ground and got the fire started.

She noticed movement in the wagon to the west of them and was pleased when she saw Patty Reed jump down from their big splendid wagon and wave to Mary. Virginia climbed down after Patty. Smiling at Mary, she and Patty, who each had a bucket, went down to the water together.

"Let us leave these buckets with Eliza and we'll come back to visit," Patty promised.

They had had some time to get to know each other and the girls were becoming fast friends.

As Virginia and Patty approached the Murphy fire, they three sat down to chat.

One of the main topics was Eddie and they were watching the Breen wagon waiting to see movement from inside. It wasn't long until they saw John Breen jump out of the wagon. Then Patrick Jr. stuck his head out and handed John two buckets. John walked by their fire to say good morning.

"Morning John!" called out Virginia. "How is Eddie this morning?"

"Morning!" called out John. "He passed a tolerably well night. He tosses and turns so usually. Miss Tamsen and Eliza have been helpful in giving him draughts to help him lie more easily." He swung his buckets and went down to the water's edge. On his way back, he looked at the three girls sitting expectantly by the fire. He knew they were wondering about Eddie and that his explanation had not been enough to satisfy their curiosity. "So I expect you want to visit Eddie and see how he is doing? Why don't you come with me and say good morning. He is awake, and Pa has gotten him dressed, so come on."

The girls followed obediently.

"Morning girls!" Mrs. Breen called from inside the wagon.

Eddie was propped up on quilts and looking pale. His injured leg wrapped in cloth strip bandages stretched out carefully in front of him. It too was raised up on quilts. They could see the leg was swollen, red, and looked painful.

"Morning Eddie," said Mary shyly.

"Eddie, how are you?" asked Patty sincerely.

"Hi," Eddie answered softly. Then he asked Virginia how the horses were. He was worried his horse had injured her leg and would have to be put down. He felt relief wash over him as Virginia responded.

"They are fine, and of course your pony is waiting for you to come back and ride her," she said. They talked more, munching on the biscuits.

Although the boy was pale, he was glad to talk with his friends. They chatted and Mrs. Breen brought them some more biscuits to eat. She stood back and watched her son nibble at the warm biscuit dripping with fresh honey they had found a few days before. He was eating, which was a good sign, and while the swelling in his leg persisted, it had not gotten worse.

Tamsen was coming by twice a day to look at his leg, treating it with some of the medicines she had brought with her. She made poultices and tea from nettles, used some nightshade and other plants to relieve the pain. Eliza from the Reed wagon had been helpful as well bringing potions for him to drink to help him sleep. Mrs. Breen was so thankful for the knowledge and the generosity of her wagon mates. She shook her head. She wasn't sure if they had made the right decision letting Eddie keep his leg. However, she also knew if they had amputated his leg and he had been so fearful and so against it, he would have died within days. He would have been so upset. She knew he would have felt betrayed by his parents and that he would probably have given up. The will to live and the need to be strong had to come from within. It did not matter now. The deed was in the past and Eddie would live or die by that decision.

She remembered how loathsome the doctor who had come out to "help" them was. She cringed as she thought of those dirty hands touching her son. *No*, she thought, *I believe we made the right decision.* She straightened her shoulders, glanced out of the wagon to gauge where the sun was. It was close to sunrise. Turning to their guests, she proclaimed, "It looks like a beautiful day today. I reckon we will have an early start, so you'd best be getting back to your wagons."

The children obediently got to their feet, and with a chorus of "thank yous," they showed gratitude to Mrs. Breen for the biscuits, and then, in tandem, swung down and went back to their wagons. Mary waved good-bye to the girls and then got the warmed bucket of water from the fire's ashes and climbed back into her wagon. Her mother and brothers were up and getting dressed. She left the warm water for them to wash up with and got ready to cook the breakfast.

August 2, 1846, The Bear River

The wagon train had chosen a camp site beyond the banks of the Little Muddy. The banks were not muddy at all and easy to climb. Patty, Elitha, Leanna, and Virginia picked beautiful pink and purple blossoms. Bringing them to Tamsen, she identified them as wild geraniums. She showed them how to break off the stems and put them in water so they would root themselves. "You don't need seeds to grow all plants," she said, "like onions and the eyes of potatoes."

Patrick Dolan, Charles Stanton, and three others "fished" in the Little Muddy. They caught bass, pike, and crappie along protected banks and in clearer water. They brought a whole line of fish for a feast that evening.

They built their campfire not far from a clear spring and filled all the water jugs with the clean, sweet water. Everyone gathered around, and playful, friendly banter could be heard from the men while cleaning the fish.

"Quite a difference from the beginning of this trail, isn't it?" inquired James Reed. He was happy to point out how smooth the trail was now and George and Jacob Donner were only too happy to agree with him. Tamsen had to admit that things were looking much better for them, but she couldn't discount her misgivings. Elizabeth Donner patted her hand and said, "It will be fine, Tamsen, there you go overthinking things. Just enjoy the trip, and have some more fish." It was delicious and they had so many fish that they smoked to eat later on in the journey. Others were put on rocks and racks to dry covering them with salt to keep the bugs away.

The group relaxed and again there was singing and storytelling.

The stop was a nice break for Luke Halloran as well. His sickness, also called Consumption, is known today as Pulmonary Tuberculosis. A disease of the lungs which becomes progressively worse robbing the body of its ability to fight off infections. Luke was experiencing the tiring disease's constant coughing, weight loss, and lack of strength. He found he became quite tired on exertion and was slowly wasting away. Although Luke was young at 25, he tried to do small chores around the campfire, but he had little energy and not the strength to be of much help. He was so worried that this group of fine people would find him a burden and leave him on the trail like the last group did. The sumptuous fish dinner was nourishing for him and easy to eat, providing good protein. The rest stop gave him an opportunity to be undisturbed. Luke gratefully curled up and slept with a full stomach.

Little Eddie Breen was also grateful for the stop. With his broken leg, every wagon jolt sent pain from his toes to the top of his head. He found it hard to keep from moaning or sometimes yelping, so he kept his quilt near his mouth so he could scream when the wagon hit a deep rut. Nonetheless, being a tough little guy, and like Luke, he was determined to continue and not be left behind. He stretched out on his pallet, stomach full, then gingerly moved his tortured limb and settled back for a nap.

Patty came by later to visit and, like Eddie's mother and Tamsen, checked his toes to make sure they were warm. Surprisingly, they were still warm, pink, and not showing signs of deadly gangrene.

As the evening progressed, the frogs quieted down, the moon rose, and soon there was no activity around the campfires. The embers burned down as everyone slept. Even the dogs slept off and on keeping their vigil and opening an eye as the breeze stirred the leaves but going back to sleep as nothing came towards the group.

August 6, The Raging Water of the Weber River

What a difference a few days make. James Reed, Jacob, and George Donner looked in dismay at the wild, raging waters. A few days ago, they were fishing from the banks, watching the lazy current in the water way. Now, they were trying to figure out how to negotiate the wild waves. Other men joined the group as they decided how to navigate the next section of the foaming water. Boulders, too huge to move, would be dangerous obstacles if they tried to sail their wagons down the river. Because of the turmoil of the water, the men decided to unhitch the teams at certain points and anchor each side in the back of every wagon with oxen to help stabilize the wagons as they maneuvered through the water. The men walked alongside turning the large wooden spokes of the wheels, pushing the wagons forward through the water. This new obstruction created another time-eating barrier. Hitching and unhitching the oxen, walking and pushing the wheels through the water, and then drying out the wagons and moving on slowed down each day's progress, and the extra work was making everyone tired. For two days, they slugged it out in the mud and raging waters coaxing the oxen and the heavy wagons forward. After the second day of pushing and pulling the wagons through the water, everyone collapsed by the side of the Weber.

Too tired to cook, they built a few campfires, dried themselves, their clothes, the dogs, and ate smoked fish for dinner. No singing, storytelling, nor dancing was heard that night. Instead, the camp was soon filled with soft snores.

August 8, Echo Canyon, Valley of the Weber

On the trail, a forward horseback rider found a stick jutting out from a sagebrush bush with a note from Hastings, what a find! Excitement buzzed up down the line of immigrants. They had heard from Hastings. He hadn't totally abandoned them. Finally, they had some news. They weren't as alone as they had thought. Things were going to get better. They stopped and crowded around as one of the men read the note.

The Weber route was bad and Hastings felt his way was better. Mr. Hastings would have to come back to show them the way through the Wasatch Mountains.   Immediately, the mood improved throughout the wagon train. At last, they would have someone lead them through the pass. They would not get lost now. Mr. Hastings would join them and he would lead them through the shortcut. The men congratulated themselves for making the right decision about the shortcut and they proceeded forward, their moods much lightened.

But when they reached the Wasatch Mountains, they were in for a nasty surprise. Again, there was no Hastings waiting for them. He had waited, believed they were taking too long to catch up to him, so Hastings had moved on. What? Hastings couldn't wait for them? He just left a whole wagon train to be on its own? How could that have happened? How could this man leave them stranded? This was his shortcut. They were following his instructions and he had said he would wait. Tempers flared. Again, the men gathered and loud arguments ensued. They all wanted someone to blame. Whose idea was it to follow Hastings? Why wasn't he there? They yelled and argued, but in the end, their cause was lost for the moment. The wagon train was hopelessly stranded again.

After finding the second note from Lansford Hasting, he advised them to stop, make camp where they were, and wait while they sent a messenger forward to him. Some discussed the idea that maybe they should go back to Fort Bridger and await Hastings there to come through again. Hastings was telling them that he wanted to re-route them because the travel through the Weber Canyon was too harsh. The group of men stared at each other wondering what nonsense this was.

"We are in the Weber Valley, we know how bad it is, and we have come this far," grumbled a man next to James Reed.

"What in tarnation is that man thinking?" yelled James Reed. "To go back to Fort Bridger we would waste more time and to wait here doesn't make sense." A feeling of panic was settling in. It was almost mid-August. Sometimes snow and rains started in September. Suddenly, they were low on time and the clock was ticking. No way could they go back!

George suggested that James, William Pike, and Charles Stanton should ride ahead and explore the canyon to determine if they could get through it or not. The three men should have been able to see if they could bring the wagons forward to continue. Then they could determine if they should turn back to the fort or not. Meanwhile, the wagon train has been forced to stop once again. There was nowhere for them to go, and so another stop was eating up precious time. The three elected men took their fastest horses and left.

Luke Halloran and Eddie Breen enjoyed the prolonged rest stop. No movement helped them sleep and, for a while, they were in no pain. The other children began to explore the area, and Tamsen, Margaret Reed, and the other women set out to make the most of the break. They washed clothes, repaired small items, and took inventory of the stores. The other men worked on wagon repairs and tried their hand at hunting.

Tamsen and Margaret confided their worries to each other. It was already August and they were nowhere near their destination. And although it is said that the California territory was the land of milk and honey, they wondered how cold and snowy a weather they may have to pass through to get there.

August 11, Echo Canyon, Valley of the Weber River

When the three men returned, they told of Reed leading the way hacking at the profuse vegetation. "It is possible to move forward," they said, "better than going back." Most of the wagon train agreed with this proposition. So they hitched up the wagons and began the very slow progression forward. Hacking their way, they wound up to a barrier. Brambles, bushes, and trees created a sticky, harsh wall that they had to push their way through. Skin on arms and legs and clothing was ripped and torn by the unwieldy branches, scratching and tearing away protective coverings. All of the children walked behind the wagons. They would push or use the back of the wagon as a crutch. They were warned when they began to walk behind the center of the wagon's back. Then if the wagon were to roll backwards, they would drop to the ground to avoid being crushed. Patty kept Tommy in front of her and Jimmy right behind her. Watching them closely to make sure their arms weren't torn by the brambles and to keep their steps solid and true. The going was very slow, but because it was slow, Patty could make sure both boys were safe. The dogs walked along staying close to the children. The trail was so narrow and choked with vegetation that the dogs didn't try running off.

At last, the wagon train came to a halt. The group breathed a collective sigh of relief as they finally fought their way through the last of the thick, miserable underbrush. Now the trail should be easier. But, what was this up ahead? A group of men were standing stock still. Jim Reed was shaking his head, George and Milt looked on with disbelief. Many sounds of dismay echoed up and down the line from every wagon. Patty lifted her eyes up. They have been brought up short by another problem: a huge stone edifice…

As the wagon train stopped, the women gazed up the huge, rocky cliffs with fear, misgivings, and disappointment. There was no trail, no indication of a way up. There were more brambles and bushes that would have to be hacked out of their way. The mountain looked like it went straight up. More cries of dismay and despair were heard.

Many sat down. Mrs. Keseberg collapsed to the ground. Holding her baby in her arms who was resting on her growing belly, she shook her head and buried her head down onto her baby's downy head moaning softly.

Patty felt fear in the pit of her stomach. *How would we get up to the top*, she wondered.

"How are we ever going to get this wagon up this mountain?" wondered Margaret Reed aloud, echoing Patty's concerns. She stepped back a step then two looking up at the massive wall of granite, rock, and prickly bushes. Her husband and other men were walking back to the desolate group of women and children. The men were tired, angry, and perplexed. They looked questioningly at James.

"Hmm," he mused. "Well, we'll unharness the oxen and use those big boulders as levers, and see those big trees? We can use them as fulcrums. With our heavy ropes, we can bring the wagons up the slope," he finished sounding cheerier than he felt. He found it hard to swallow and worried at such a labor-intensive project. Could they really get these heavy wagons up and over this mountain? He took another swallow. "How about I take the ropes and some men up there and set about getting us ready to hoist the wagons up this face?" he called out to George Donner.

Milt stood up and nodded. "Yes, we can do this; it is going to take a little bit of time. But the oxen are strong and they can pull."

Tamsen put her arm on George's arm and smiled encouragingly to him all the while wondering if they were doomed.

"Think we can get everyone up there?" George asked eyeing the steep slopes of rock and brush.

"I believe I can, George." James set about gathering ropes and leather straps. He directed the others how to disengage the oxen yokes and store them in bundles to be hoisted up. Organizing the men into groups, they decided among themselves who would go up first, who would help guide the suspended wagons, oxen, and cows on the way up, and who would monitor and help push everything up the embankment. It would be quite a production and, of course, would take all day and maybe longer to get all of the wagons up.

Immediately, the group swung into action. Men were collecting the ropes and unhitching the oxen. The women started figuring out how to secure and maybe lighten the wagons.

Elitha, Leanna, Mary Donner, Mary Graves, Patty, and Virginia helped tie down moveable objects inside the wagons. George, Patrick, Eddie, John, and Simon helped with moving heavier things and the animals to get them ready for the upward trip.

Tamsen was addressing the girls, "Would you take care of the little ones and help them up this incline? I think there are enough of you to carry the babies and help with some of the older and more delicate women." She looked at Mrs. Keseberg pregnant and with a small child in her arms.

"Please, Mrs. Keseberg, let us help you carry the baby," Margaret urged her kindly. The woman hesitated and then gratefully handed her child to Margaret. With Virginia walking alongside, the three women set out to climb the rocky, slippery mountain.

August 12, The Wasatch Mountains

The wall of mountains loomed before them. Although spectacular and possibly the most beautiful part of the Rocky Mountains, it was also the most treacherous. Small, narrow twisting canyons led the group over rocky terrain and continually upwards. Often times, they found themselves switching back on a trail to where they started. Frustrations climbed and tempers were short. It was all Patty could do to keep up with the group even though she walked with the younger two boys. Jagged rocks and their sharp, uneven surfaces cut through their shoes. Cries of pain, frustration, and anger were heard up and down the straggling line as someone slipped, cursed, or cried as they stumbled over the miserable, unforgiving ground. Despite the agony of the climb, the children bore the treacheries of the days with little complaint. They looked forward to coming down the other side of the mountain and the possibility of a ride. The canyon rivers flowed with water, but often these waterfalls were far from their reach.

Night after night, they stopped sooner than sundown. Everyone was grateful for the respite from the hiking. The continual upwards pushing of the wagons, the oxen, the horses, and the pioneers caused swollen knees, sore bleeding feet, worn out shoe soles, and aching backs. The uneven trail was taking its toll.

"Let us hope this is the worst that we will endure," Margaret Reed said hoping she was sounding positive to her children. She looked around at her children. They sat quietly eating their dinner looking forward to sleeping and not walking.

Margaret and Tamsen had spoken earlier. They were both aware that the days were getting shorter. Sunset came sooner. They were stopping earlier now because of the degree of difficulty in each day. Already, they could feel the fall chill in the air. Time was getting shorter. Soon, the first snows would arrive. Nevertheless, they had comforted each other; the snows usually came in December. The west coast promised warmer, milder weather. Surely, the snows would not come early! Even if they were delayed, they would be in the Sacramento Valley before the first snowfall. Then they would be all right.

August 16, 1846,
The Graves Family Joins the Wagon Train

"Haw!" shouted Franklin Graves. He did see wagons ahead. *What luck*, he thought hoping the wagons in front of him were indeed the Donner wagons. They themselves were a group of 13 men and children with three wagons. One of their wagons was a "special" one. Drilled into the sideboards of it were stacks of silver coins. Mr. Graves had been told a large wagon train was ahead of them and he had hoped they could overtake them. He had left Illinois although a native of Vermont. He loved the adventure of the open road and had enticed his family to accompany him with wild tales of wonder about the new lands of the west. His wife, Elizabeth, smiled and laughed when they caught up with the other wagons. In fact, everyone enjoyed the company of Elizabeth Graves. She had a sunny disposition and was always smiling. Everyone looked to Elizabeth for an encouraging word or a sympathetic and nice thing to say. The children loved to listen to her stories and she had the most beautiful daughter, Mary Ann Graves. Also traveling with them was their teamster, John Snyder. John Snyder was sweet with Mary Ann. He was very happy to have been chosen as a work-hand for the Graves. He liked the family and *especially* Mary Ann. They liked to spend time together. Mary Ann was shy and not aware of what a beauty she was. She had a quick smile and was kind to everyone. *But there is something special about that John Snyder*, she thought.

The Graves also brought several head of cattle with them, fresh, strong oxen, and they were laden with supplies. They were welcomed with open arms by Donner party train. Now they numbered 87 with 22 wagons.

*   *   *   *   *

William Graves, Franklin's son, would later blame James Reed for forcing them to take the shortcut road to Salt Lake. Even though he wasn't with the wagon train when they made the decision to split.

August 24, 1946

Coming down the southeast side towards the Great Salt Lake, one of the Reed's wagons broke an axle. They had to stop and wait while two men from the wagon train rode fifteen miles away back up the mountain to find any timber to repair the axle. Another day was lost. Margaret could feel the summer slipping away. But when Patty voiced her concern, her mother attempted to allay her fears. "We are moving slowly now, but we will pick up speed. Remember, this is a shortcut, and soon we will be moving along," Margaret spoke with lightness she had to force.

They had spent yesterday inching up a mountain that required them to hitch all of the oxen to one cart at a time to get it up the mountain. Now, they were on the other side and stalled forced to go back up to the timber line. Fate was not smiling upon them. Time indeed was slipping away.

Virginia overheard her father talking with her mother. He complained that it took 18 days to travel 30 miles. They left Fort Bridger and thought they were about seven weeks from Sutter's Fort. Now, they were forced to slow down again. They still needed to get to the other side of the Great Salt Lake and they were still more than 720 miles from where they could stop. "I ask you, Margaret, what are we going to do? I am worried about the extra time. I agreed to this so called shortcut and now I am beginning to agree with Tamsen. We may have made a bad mistake. I am hoping the rest of the trail is easier."

Margaret was worried as well. Some of the people of the wagon train were becoming weaker from hunger and lack of food and water. They were definitely moving slower. Each day, they made such little progress that the weight of their sad situation became heavier and heavier. Nerves became frayed and raw and erupted into angry outbursts at the slightest provocation. As they contemplated their strife, they wanted to blame someone. Whose fault was this? Feelings of goodwill were gone. As they wondered whose "fault" it was, they decided that it had to be the fault of Mr. Reed's. James Reed was their scapegoat. It was *his* idea to take the shortcut. *Him and his airs*, many thought. He also had the bigger, heavier fancy wagons. *His* huge wagons were slower wagons, weaker by their immense size, and more prone to breaks needing repairs. For the first time, fear of being lost and fear of so many more days of hard, dangerous traveling began to make these emigrants worry. They were, as a group now, starting to worry about the weather. Casting an eye to the sky, they could sense the change in weather. The end of summer was coming and they still had hundreds of miles to travel. Moreover, who knew what other folly might befall them?

While these delays were treacherous, they were deadly for poor

Luke Halloran. He became weaker and weaker. His interest in life on the wagon train ceased. He could no longer care for himself. He was now very dependent upon George and Tamsen Donner for his every need. He died with his head on Tamsen's lap. They had to stop and bury him in that God forsaken country. For that misery, there was the loss of a half-day.

August 27, the Salt Lake Valley

Fifteen days later, the thirty-six miles took them so long to traverse that the Grave, Stanton, and McCuthen parties had caught up with the larger group. Now, they found themselves in woods of aspens, poplars, and cottonwoods. The underbrush was so dense it took hours to hack through the heavy, low branches and bushes. Arms and legs were again lacerated, scraped, and cut. Bleeding arms were tended to, but as they became so numerous, they often didn't bother. Shredded sleeves offered little protection. Many of the pioneers, men, women, and children sported long sleeves, skirts, and pant legs that were ripped and spotted with red.

Patty looked at George in his long sleeved, light poplin shirt. It was now streaked with red. She almost called out to him and as she raised her hand to her mouth, she realized her long sleeves were just as stripped with her blood.

Another cumbersome barrier were the boulders. Huge and small rocks, all sharp, blockaded every step. Then there were the heavy, smelly, bug infested swamps and brooks. Their feet were soaked in the dirty, foul smelling water. Swarms of mosquitoes flew like a moving veil in front of their eyes. When they brushed away the high-pitched blankets of bugs, the flies flew at them trying to get in their eyes, ears, noses, and mouths. Coughing and spitting noises were heard. Bugs were discharged out of their mouths and noses. When they finally had managed to make it through one small area, they had to scale inclines, which were rock walls. These rested on a base of gravel and for every two steps up they tried, they slid back one step. The trail was so difficult. Three times they found themselves at an impassable barrier and then they had to trudge back and restart. Fifteen days of loose rock walls, boulders, swamps, and restarts found the emigrants tiring and losing their strength. They retraced their steps returning to the start point and fording off in different directions only to enter another canyon and try their luck there. They entered canyon after canyon. Finally, at last, they found the correct canyon to lead them to Valley of the Lake.

Again, the countryside had changed dramatically. The aspens and poplars of the canyons and the dense underbrush could not be supported here. The trail was so hot and the countryside desolate. Everywhere was hot, dry, burning sand. There were no trees, no grass, and only a few scrub bushes that were so dry and brown that they disintegrated with a simple touch.

September 1, the Great Salt Lake

As they stood looking over the huge Salt Lake, there was nothing but flatness of land and the beige colored sand and wisps of scraggly plants. And it was hot. Clouds of black bugs swarmed over the water. It was hot and it stank. Clothes stuck to their hot skin. They put handkerchiefs over their faces to avoid the stink and the bugs.

"What is this horrid place?" asked Eliza. She looked with shock and dismay at what lay ahead of them.

The Great Salt Lake overstrained Eliza. She and almost every other person in the group felt fear, exhaustion, and oppressive heat. The group was quick to anger, and the condition of the animals worsened by the hour. They were tired, thirsty, and hungry. Pulling the huge burdens that they had day after day was taking its toll on the beasts.

Patty, Virginia, George, and Eddie, now walking without a crutch, slowly followed the wagons.

"It is so hot," complained George.

Patty only nodded. Her mouth was so dry. Her lips cracked and she no longer had any spit to wet her lips. She took in a breath of hot, stale air. Gone were the beautiful green trees. She missed seeing the brilliant green leaves of the cottonwoods that grew along the creeks and rivers. Every time she had seen those trees in a line, she knew there was water. Now there was none. She missed the cool breeze coming down from the canyons. She held Tommy's hot little hand and told him stories to keep him occupied while they marched slowly onward.

Tommy's red face peeked out from his wide brimmed hat. He listlessly allowed himself to be pulled along by Patty. Cash, his dog, followed loyally. He too was hot and thirsty and did not run ahead as he used to. He walked in step with the children, his tongue hanging out the side of his mouth. The group concentrated on the act of walking, putting one foot in front of the other.

Eddie, although just as hot and tired as the others, was glad to be walking on his own. Had he been using his crutch, it would have sunk into the sand with each step he took. *I may not be walking very fast in this sand, he thought, but I am walking on my own two legs. Anyways, no one else is walking too quickly.* He occupied himself by thinking of the fun things he would do when they reached Sacramento. He kept his eye on Patty and Tommy, making sure not to fall too far behind.

The progress of the wagon train was slower and slower. Bogged down by the sand and the fierce heat, they traveled more in the early morning and late evening camping during the hottest part of the day trying to avoid the broiling sun. Because of the oppressive heat, they weren't able to rest even when they stopped. The children had dark circles under their eyes, red faces, and blistered, peeling lips and foreheads.

Virginia's bonnet was fraying. The ends had been baked and were faded. The part that used to come over her face and provide shade was worn and torn. Her throat was dry too and it hurt to talk. Keeping her head down, she trudged along the sandy way.

The burning sand radiated heat. It was dry heat, oppressively dry heat that lay on the body like a heavy wool blanket. It was the kind of dry heat that sucked the moisture from the skin, mouth, and nose of every living creature on the trail. Shirts, although providing protection from the sun, scraped, rubbed raw, and irritated dry skin. Reddened, blistered skin rubbed raw from walking split open and became infected. Mary thought back to the cold and continuously wet earlier days and sighed. She had hated the cold, wet weather and had wished for the heat. Now, she hated the heat. What had her father said? "Be careful for what you wish for." He was so right. Would they ever cool down?

After five days in Skull Valley, *wasn't that an appropriate name to call this God forsaken place,* mused Eliza to herself, they were at last at the Oasis east of the Great Salt Lake. Nothing but sand–hot, bug infested sand–stretched out before them.

What did she spy? Tamsen, glad to be roused from her thoughts and the drudgery of walking, reached out into the tangled brush. Fragments of paper tangled in and on bushes were scattered about the trail. Pieced together by Tamsen, she saw that Hastings had written them. As she read the scrawled messages, she realized she had been right. This Left Hand Turn that they had taken, this "so called shortcut," would be longer in execution. He wrote that it would take a little longer. What an exaggeration that turned out to be! In actuality, it was two days and two nights longer. This horrid desert was sucking the life out of the Donner/Reed party and their livestock.

The blinding desert sand blew into their eyes. The hot, smothering winds blew against their bodies and robbed their skin and eyes of moisture. Blinking an eye was gritty and painful. Dry mouths yearned for moisture. Blisters appeared on feet, broke, and then became painful in chafed areas. The need for water made their thirst agonizing. They could only travel at night because to travel during the day would mean certain death. There was fear that they might die here in this life sucking, miserable desert never to reach California.

By now, the wagon train stretched for almost a mile. Sometimes, it would take an hour or more of walking to catch up with the main part of the train. As mishaps happened, families were left behind.

Sometimes taking hours to catch up, in the dark, after the main group had stopped for the night. If someone were to have severe problems, the rest of the pioneers may never know what happened.

The main group continued on until they found the watering hole. They threw themselves into the water sharing the cool wetness with the animals.

The heavily loaded wagons of the Reeds lagged in the rear. By the third day, they had no water left. They had to stop. The rest of the wagon train was so far ahead, they could see no sign of them. James Reed rode forward to the group ahead, hoping for water. He tried to trade the things they had for it. Now, no one cared for his silver, china, or his glassware. James was finding no takers to trade with him. The pioneers found they had to start lightening the loads that they were carrying. At this time, so many of the pioneers were at the point of abandoning their wagons in total that they were actually considering leaving their entire wagonloads of goods and continue by foot. All of their household goods, their treasures, keepsakes, and clothing, they were planning to leave it all just so they could leave this God-forsaken, hot, miserable land. All of their treasures that would have made the new territory their home, they were now thinking of leaving in the desert. Gone would be the beautifully carved dressers, chairs, lovely stitched stools. Dishes, silverware, family heirlooms were now buried, or "cached," left sitting by the trail. They had reached the point where no one cared what they left. They were more concerned about being able to continue walking. They worried about surviving the awfulness of the desert.

September 2

After six days of looking for lost cattle, the Reeds finally prepared to catch up with the group.

"I will ride ahead and see where the next water source is," James Reed said to his tired, hot, listless family. "I think the rest of the group is already there."

The Reeds gathered around their wagon. Tommy climbed under the wagon to get out of the heat and the others followed. They would wait there for their father to get back with the precious water.

September 3

After two days, James Reed indeed found the rest of the Donners at the lovely, cool spring at the base of Pilot Peak. Everyone was enjoying the water. It was replenishing their dry, hard, cracked, bloodied skin. Some found that they could drink and still feel thirsty. Canteens, buckets, any containers, some already full of other foods, were dumped to be filled with the precious commodity of wetness. Horses, dogs, and oxen walked into the water and took long drinks.

Mr. Reed filled up with water and set out to return to his family. He passed Milford Elliot who was driving the team of oxen to the water hole.

"You watch them, Milt," he said nodding to the oxen. "As soon as they smell the water, they will stampede."

Milt nodded and gave a wave as they passed each going in separate directions.

James Reed waited with the family all that day for Milt to return. He did not. They decided to start walking towards the spring. They would come back for their goods. They started out with the five dogs, Patty, Virginia, Tommy, Jimmy, and Margaret. Dusk fell soon and fierce wind had begun to blow. They gathered in a circle and James covered them with blankets.

Not long into the night, the dogs started barking alerting them of an attack.

James looked up to see several huge animals, lowing loudly and snorting, lumbering towards them. As they drew near, two of the dogs attacked the mass of beasts and forced them to change direction. More came trampling in. Then they realized they were their own cattle.

September 4

By the fourth day of traveling forward from the Oasis, they had no more water. Stranded again, the group was powerless to move any longer. They couldn't go forward without some liquid. The oxen and horses were weak and hard to control. The whites of their eyes showed and the slightest movement would terrify the beasts. As they reached Pilot Peak, the beasts of burden could smell the water. The smell of water, coupled with the animals being so tired and pushed to their limit, made them uncontrollable. Wild, unreasonable, and near death, they tried to make a break in the direction of the water. A few animals had torn loose from their harnesses. They were running heedlessly towards their salvation.

James Reed was returning to the wagon train from going ahead to meet with the unprincipled Hastings. He was carrying water, riding back to his wagons. He met the scene of wild and loose oxen with an instant understanding. The oxen were close to death. He had encouraged the handlers earlier on as he went up and down the wagon train talking to the teamsters to unhitch the oxen and allow them to go for water on their own. That did not happen. The oxen stampeded; maddened by thirst and the promise of water by its smell, they tore through the remains of the wagon train. Confused and irrational, the beasts crashed through the area scattering in all directions.

Delayed and far back from the group, the Reed family didn't know what was happening. They were walking on foot now; they had no wagons and had very few possessions. They walked at night to avoid the burning rays of the sun. Mr. Reed carried Tommy. Margaret, Virginia, and Patty were carrying what food and water they had. They walked until they were too tired to move. Finally collapsing on the ground, they stayed where they were, covered themselves with blankets, and fell asleep.

Suddenly, awakened by a thundering noise, they sat up. The earth shook. Abruptly, huge, dark shapes breathing hard stomped into their small camp. Tommy cried out and Virginia screamed. Margaret grabbed Jimmy and swept him aside as a wild ox threw his head and horns in the air, mucous flying from the enraged beast's mouth as he roared in frustration. The insane oxen were charging at them. Barely avoiding trampling by sharp hooves, they scrambled away from the watered-crazed beasts. As they trampled on, Margaret and James took stock of the family. Everyone was present and unharmed.

Slowly, they gathered their meager possessions and began to walk. They walked in silence until they reached Jacob Donner's wagon. He allowed them to sleep there in their wagon. The next day, they scouted for the lost oxen. They rested and took six days to look for the rest of the beasts of burden and to repose.

Thirty-six oxen, half of them belonging to the Reeds, died or stampeded that night. Gone were most of the oxen and cattle. What an awful mess this was.

The Reeds were left with nothing to pull all of their wagons. With just an ox and a cow remaining alive, they had to make some hard decisions. Therefore, they were forced to scuttle two of the wagons. Gone now was the beautiful and huge Palace car. They were down to one wagon. It had been difficult to leave so many of their beautiful things. China, silver, dressers, their iron stove, chairs, beds, books, treasures, and all these things had to be left behind. Most of their furniture and property were buried in the sand, but some were left strewn on the side of the trail. As they had become more tired and embittered, and finally, not even caring if their goods were buried or cached, they left their treasures where they fell. The fortune of the Reeds was almost non-existent. James was hoping to preserve the last wagon by purchasing some oxen from one of the other wagon train members.

Patty was very practical about their loss. "Now Jimmy," she instructed, "our travels will be easier because we don't have to worry about all of our things. We need to concentrate on walking and staying together." She took Jimmy and Tommy by their hands and began a long tiring walk in the dark. Virginia followed slowly with her mother and the dogs trailing behind.

James went to Patrick Breen to buy two oxen to allow his remaining ox and cow to pull his wagon. He had distributed his remaining supplies sharing the food and left over tins with the others in the wagon train, especially giving the best to Patrick. Patrick had not wanted to give away his oxen, but he knew how desperate James was and his family could use the food, so he sold him the oxen.

The days progressed with a mind numbing sameness. The group got up and moved the wagon train out. Those who were not driving the oxen and those who were able walked. They stopped briefly for the midday meal and then continued walking until suppertime. They no longer got together for the community bonfire at night. Everyone was tired and wanted to sleep. If forced to admit it, they didn't feel so friendly with one another, and the less time they spent together they thought the better.

Down to the Humboldt they walked. More oxen died and they continued to lighten the loads. On good days, everyone buried their treasures hoping to come back for them. Maps and narratives were written and dictated so they would know where to return for their goods... On bad days, however, when they were so tired, they had to leave items to lighten the load on the roadside. Then other travelers or Indians could take the discarded goods. Dwindling food was also becoming a problem. Many a night, Patty would sing softly to her brothers encouraging them to sleep, hoping they might find more food the next day along the bitter trail. But knowing in her heart, they would not find anything to eat. They would soon begin their ascent to the Sierras and the fear of snow, blizzards, and frozen ground would be their next challenge. The changes for the fall season were beginning to be noticed.

September 18, 1846

The lessening amount of food available to all the members of the Donner party was indeed becoming worrisome. The men got together and decided that Mr. Stanton and Mr. McCuthen would ride on to Sutter's fort in the Sacramento Valley for food and provisions. They figured that two men would make good time and they could bring back donkeys laden with food. Off they went with much fanfare and for the next few days, everyone was heartened by the idea of some kind of nourishment coming to them soon.

Once again, for a few nights, the group got together for nightly campfires. Virginia, Patty, Mary, and the other girls sang and danced to the harmonica playing. The boys with the sharpened sticks imagining going out and hunting for game with dreams of supplying the whole wagon train with enough food for dinner and the next day. But the next day, reality returned. The weather was cooler and wetter.

Slogging through the trail now was slow going. The wagon's cumbersome, wooden wheels became mired in mud and clay. Some of the wood in the wheels split or the iron covering the wheel slipped off. It was difficult to repair and if it couldn't be done, the wagon was left and the goods in the wagon distributed among other wagons or horses. Where they were, there was water everywhere. Water splashed down the sides of the rocky cliffs like miniature waterfalls. The trees, dark, green leaves and needles dripped with rainwater. In the beginning, the coolness of the water felt good and was a welcome relief. Then the water became ever present. There were narrow gaps along the trail and vertical cliffs that climbed straight up towards the sky. When they were on somewhat flat land, there was stinking quicksand. It was dark brown and had a peculiar stench. Mosquitoes and flies surrounded the liquid ground.

Virginia and Patty slapped at the insects as they dive-bombed them. They were wet and their clothes stuck to them. If they had noticed, they would have seen that their dresses, which once were hard to fasten, were now becoming looser on their bodies. They were always hungry and tired at the end of the day. Hot water was boiled for baths in the evening and even Tommy and Jimmy didn't complain when they were told to wash themselves.

Another difference was in the Indians they saw. These Indians looked thin and hungry. They did not wear many clothes. They were constantly following the impaired wagon train. They seemed to know these emigrants were in trouble and struggling. They bided their time and when someone was not paying attention to the livestock or a wagon, they swooped in and stole horses. Sometimes, a dog that was lagging behind was eventually found to be missing. The Indians became bolder as the tired and badgered pioneers ignored them. They would ride up to the side of the wagons and bravely cut a rope off the side of a wagon or a bucket or a ladle. Tamsen noticed with dismay that their bucket was no longer there. They shot arrows at the oxen hoping to wound and slow them down or to stop the wagons. One thing you could count on as you looked around, a starving Indian would be skulking about in the periphery.

October 5, 1845, The Incident

October 5 was the day the Donner-Reed wagon train was found at the bottom of a very steep mountain.

The mountain loomed hugely ahead of them. The men in the lead wagons gazed up the rocky incline. The ground was semi-soft and rocks and debris tumbled down after the initial effort to climb up. They decided to double-team each wagon to get up the steep cliff, which would provide double the extra strength needed to get the heavy wagons up and over the mountain.

They set about securing each wagon and its contents and then hitching up two teams so that the wagons could make it up the steep wall.

Mr. Eddy joined the Reeds to help them out. On the way up the hill, they met John Snyder. His wagon had stalled and he was brutally whipping the oxen. Milton Elliott shouted to him to stop. John yelled back at him to mind his own business and he could very well drive the team himself. Milt tried to get John to calm down and quit whipping the oxen, which were becoming restless. The two men got into a shouting match and John Snyder raised his whip and threatened Milt. At this point, James Reed interceded. He'd be damned if he would stand by and watch this inexperienced, nasty driver beat his oxen and his friend, Milt. He jumped into the fray.

Snyder grabbed his bullwhip and whacked James on his head. His forehead started to bleed and Margaret rushed to her husband's side. John whipped Margaret in the face and she fell to the side. Virginia screamed. Enraged, James picked up a knife and stabbed Snyder once. Immediately, Snyder fell. Without making any sounds, he simply collapsed and...died.

Eerie silence descended as James stared shocked at John Snyder. He bent down on his knees and cradled John's head. He couldn't believe that he was dead. It happened so quickly. They were angry, tempers flared, and now, this. He looked down at the face of the dead man in his lap. Someone ran to get Mr. Graves. Those who came running carried the body of John Snyder back to the Graves wagon. The whole wagon train erupted with noise and confusion.

Mary Ann Graves heard the commotion and saw a group of men carrying someone to her family's wagon. She hurried down to see what was happening.

"Oh, Mary Ann. I am so sorry to say that John Snyder has been killed." Virginia looked stricken as Mary pushed past her.

Mary Ann walked to the wagon and saw the form of John Snyder lying face up, arms at his side. His shirt was mostly red from blood loss. He was so pale and, as she touched his cheek, cold. Mary pulled back her hand and looked at her fingertips. They would never caress his cheek again. She looked up at her father and mother.

"Leave him, I will wash his body and get him ready for burial." She then set about getting water, clean clothes, and soap to care for the body.

Patty grabbed Virginia's hand and squeezed it. "Oh, Puss, what will we do? I know he was going to be her beau. She will hate us forever." Patty put her hands to her face as she cried.

With tears running down her cheek, Virginia patted her sister. "I am worried too. Pa didn't mean to kill him, but kill him, he did. I don't know how anyone is going to feel about us now." Virginia was also worried because of the words of anger exchanged between her father and Mr. Keseberg. He had routinely beaten his young wife. Virginia's father had approached Mr. Keseberg and demanded he stop beating her or he would be forced to leave the group. The beating stopped, but there was much ill will and negativity expressed by the chastised Keseberg.

The wagon train separated into two groups. One was led by Mr. Keseberg who wanted instant justice. Keseberg went as far as to raise the prop of his wagon tongue straight up into the air providing gallows in which to hang James Reed. He claimed, "Ye Court is now in session."

Many were horrified at the venom in which he spoke. Reason prevailed and the men talked him into lowering his gallows. Now, everyone was uneasy. Too quickly the camp had disintegrated into chaos.

After bandaging James' head and tending to Margaret who nursed the growing bruise on her face, calm slowly returned to the group. Soon, after much discussion, it was decided that James Reed must be banned from the wagon train. Mr. Keseberg was still grumbling about the special treatment that the rich Mr. Reed received while John Snyder lay cold. He remained unappeased and appealed to the group to institute a stronger punishment. Again, the men met to decide the fate of the murderer. The verdict was that not only would James Reed not return to the wagon train, but he was to be banned without any weaponry or food. Some people were glad to see the backside of this arrogant man. Others feared that they were losing their best leader and provider. George Donner was a wonderful man, but he was much older and was having frequent bouts with illness and was not as robust as he had been once. Again, there was a split in feelings of those in the wagon train. Some felt justice had been served, others vehemently disagreed.

James Reed left unceremoniously. Those who thought the decision was right turned their backs on him. Those who thought the punishment was too harsh and felt that self-defense was an explainable reason for the death of Mr. Snyder would not dare meet his eyes as he left.

Virginia was so upset. Distressed by the counsel's decision, she felt she had to do something to help her father. They were going to throw out her father into the wild with no provisions and, worst of all, without a firearm. How would he protect himself? After tending to her mother, she developed a plan in her mind. She searched about for food, grabbing bread, cheese, a tin of peaches, some dried buffalo and tied it up in a cloth. She unhooked a rifle and put a box of shells in her pocket. Looking around, and seeing no one watching her, she rode out with the rifle and food to find her outcast father. When she found him, she flew off her horse, crying, "Father, Father! I can't bear for you to be banned from us. You must promise to take care of yourself. Leave us notes so we know you are all right."

James Reed looked in amazement at his daughter. She had ridden all this way, by herself, to bring him food and a rifle. Tears stung his eyes. How he loved his Virginia! He promised her he would be careful and would leave them notes and signs that he was indeed fine. He assured her he would do all she asked. A tear escaped his eye as he watched her leave him. Maybe this would be the last time he ever saw her.

The next morning, the Donner party started moving again.

Mary Graves slowly walked behind the wagon. She didn't notice the clouds of dust swirling around her face. She had bathed the body of her unclaimed loved one. He would never know that she had wanted him to be her beau. She wondered what else would happen on this wretched trip.

October 7, 1846

The atmosphere had now changed in the Donner Party. Many of the wagon families were not talking to each other. They started to hoard food. People distrusted one another. Many felt taken in by trusting James Reed. Others felt that it had been self defense and that James had been treated unfairly. Some were horrified at the immediate violence voiced by some of the men. This was no longer a cohesive wagon train. Families were beginning to isolate themselves from each other.

A new problem was developing. As they entered the higher country, a different Indian clan emerged. These Indians were crafty, persistent, and always seemed to be watching. They also appeared thinner, malnourished, and wore tattered, dirty clothing. *The Nevada Indians are so different from the plains Indians*, Patty noted. These Indians seemed to mutter to themselves and didn't have the fancy headdresses or any clothing or body coverings. They seemed weak and unhealthy. But they were quite handy at procuring what they needed. They stole the Graves' horses, eighteen oxen, and one cow. She didn't think they were very nice either. They would playfully shoot at the oxen and twenty-one oxen had died or were useless because of infected wounds and broken legs. So the emigrants had to kill their own oxen and cattle and salvage what meat they could. They had been forced into a slaughter in which they would forever regret the meat they left behind. The Indians would profit by that meat.

October 13, The Humboldt River and the Sink

More and more wagons were stopping and abandoning their treasures. Silver, china, furniture, anything that can't be eaten were buried with a hope that they may return and retrieve their goods later on. Mr. Wolfinger wanted to stop again and hide his cache. He was rumored to have many gold coins. This time, the group denied his request and the wagon train moved on. Only Mr. Wolfinger and two others who remained to help him stayed behind.

Tamsen stared at her books. She wrapped them in cloth and lovingly laid them in holes in the earth. She had brought these books so she could open her "polite academy for girls." Now, they were digging holes in the dirt and hiding them in the ground. One more group of beloved items was cached into the ground. She hoped that they would be able to come back and collect their things. Everything was so different now. She remembered the camaraderie when they first began their trip. "An adventure and new beginnings," George had said, "a place to start a new school with so many students we'd have to turn them away." He had laughed. *He isn't laughing now,* she thought. No one was laughing these days. Tamsen wiped the dirt from her hands as she left the burial site of her books. It felt to her like someone had died. For Tamsen, a piece of her did die with the loss of her books. *The establishment of my school would probably be delayed*, she thought.

The Eddy family was now walking. His pockets full of lump sugar and bullets. He carried his son and his wife carried the baby.

October 14, What will be called Brady's Hot Springs

Everyone in the wagon train had grown distrustful of the others. Things were only getting worse. The Eddy family was a case in point. Mr. Eddy, having lost his oxen and one wagon, had only the clothes on his back and some lump sugar in his pockets. Those shared room with bullets. He carried his gun in one hand and his son in the other arm. William Eddy had James, a three-year old boy, whom he carried, and a one-year old baby girl named Margaret. Eleanor, his wife, who was carrying Margaret, realized what a horrible predicament they were in with no food, no water, and both of them were on foot. She began to beg from others for the precious fluid. Wouldn't someone have just a little water they could spare? It wasn't for her, it was for her babies. Because there was no water, Mr. Breen didn't want to give away any excess of the liquid. He refused to share any of his water. He felt he only had enough left for his family and his family came first. Eleanor Eddy was becoming frantic. What could they do? She fretted and worried that her babies were going to die not caring that the same would happen to her.

William Eddy heard the calling of geese as they flew over-head. He left his family and tracked the source of the sound. Slowly, he came upon the clearing where they were. They clustered in two groups honking at each other. He could see one feathered mass pecking at the ground, plunging their beaks into the softened area around cattails, spooning up grubs. He couldn't see the others. The group in front of him ignored him as he crept up to them. With a stroke of luck and the stupidity of the geese, William caught nine of them. He came back triumphantly to the group. His wife was so happy that they had food for now more than others had and this would be a grand bargaining chip for them. William distributed some of the fresh meat to everyone. He then traded some of the geese for water and other food stuffs. Feeling satisfied and proud that he could provide for his family, the Eddy foursome traveled on and there was peace in his family again. William Eddy didn't know that the cattails which had attracted the geese were also a good source of protein. The Paiutes had subsisted on cattails for hundreds of years.

They approached the Truckee River better known to them as the "Truckey." It was fairly early in the day, but the group decided it was time for some rest. They had crossed the forty-mile desert. They would enjoy their geese and then continue the next day.

The Donner party had now separated into two groups, with the second group being about a day behind the first. The news had filtered back to the second group that Mr. Wolfinger had been shot by the Indians. Two other men, Mr. Spitzer and Mr. Reinhardt, who had stayed to help him bury his money, were also shot at, but they had escaped.

Evil doings, thought George Donner. He had misgivings about the reported death. He wondered, as did many of the others in both groups, if poor Mr. Wolfinger had been murdered for his coins. Who was to know other than the two men?

October 19, Truckee Meadows, Together Again

The wagon train groups had finally joined-up again. They stopped and everyone shared what was new, what hardships they were dealing with. The children had missed each other and were quite keen to visit. The day only got better.

Oh, what a joyous day this turned out to be! Patty hugged herself with delight as she saw Charles Stanton riding into camp. He was back from Sutter's fort and with food—glorious food! He returned with seven pack-mules laden with food stuffs and two Indians by his side. Oh the wonderment in what was packed on those seven mules! So many families were down to near nothing and the idea of having rice, flour, meat, beans, coffee, and tea was too wonderful to think about.

"Where was Mr. McCuthen? Big Mac? Didn't he make it?"

"Oh, he made it all right to Sutter's Fort, but he's laid up now and couldn't make the trip back. That's why these two Indians, Luis and Salvador, came with me."

Luis and Salvador were two Catholic Miwoks who agreed to accompany Stanton and help with the relief.

Stanton also brought news that James Reed had made it to Sutter's Fort.

Oh what joyous news that was to Margaret! Her husband was safe and well. What excitement there was when she told the children that their father was alive. She hugged all the bobbing heads as they danced and laughed with relief and joy. The knowledge that he was at the fort meant that they would be seeing him soon. That evening, all those in the first group gathered together and laughed and talked and enjoyed some of the provisions that Mr. Stanton had brought.

The wagon train bogged down with extra nights of rest and time spent repairing or refurbishing wagons that didn't really need the extra work. By the time they were ready to leave, it had been snowing softly.

"We'll go tomorrow," had been the promise. The next day, it snowed harder and they were not able to move the wagons.

October 23, 1846, Tragedy

While preparing to go to Sutter's Fort with his brother-in-law, William Foster, for provisions for the re-united group, William Pike handed Mr. Foster his pepperbox pistol. Notoriously known for being unreliable, the pistol went off shooting Pike in the back as he bent down to get wood for the morning campfire. Poor Mr. Pike lingered for two hours and then died. Death was happening more frequently to the pioneers and his passing was only one more sad event. William Pike was buried in the snow.

October 25, 1846,
The Donners Are Left at the Meadow

The Breens were the lead wagon as the remaining wagons began the arduous trip up the Sierras. With the Breens were Patrick Dolan, the Kesebergs, and the Eddys–who did not have a wagon. Miles behind them were the Reed, Grave, and Murphy families. The Donners were left behind in the meadow.

October 27, 1846

George Donner smiled and patted Tamsen's hand. He was in the lead wagon with Jacob following behind them. Suddenly, as they were crossing a very steep bank, the wagon overturned breaking an axle.

Violently thrown to the ground, Tamsen screamed. She turned frantically and tried to see the children through the jumble of the wagon and thrashing beasts of burden. Elitha and Leanna were walking alongside the wagon. Quickly they sprang into action to help their parents find little Georgia, four, and three-year-old Eliza. They could hear whimpering from among the thick wall of quilts and blankets. Elitha pushed her arm in the mound of heavy material and found the hand of Georgia. She pulled out her crying sister. Tamsen found Eliza and brought the terrified baby to her arms.

"What now?" questioned George as he grabbed an ax. He climbed a hill and chopped down a tree to get wood to fix the axle. As he chopped the wood to fashion an axle shaft, the chisel slipped and sliced deeply into his hand. George screamed as the blood spurted.

Tamsen gasped and rushed to him. Elitha saw the accident and ran with a square of cloth. Tamsen ripped it into strips and bounded the bloody hand.

"See what I will do to get out of work? Don't worry, my love, this is no more than a scratch and nothing to worry about." He kissed the top of her head. "Don't look so worried," he chided Elitha and Leanna as they stared at the injured hand. He waved his bandaged hand. "Nothing to worry about. Now let us continue."

With Jacob's help, they were unable to repair the axle. "We'll finish it tomorrow and then be on our way," promised George. However, the next morning extended into afternoon and they were still repairing the axle when the winds and snow blew down from Alaska starting the long, cold, snowy stretch soon to be known as the Donner Winter.

They could not repair the wagon and as the days grew colder and windier. And as the snows began, they decide to hunker down. They built tent lean-tos using blankets and hides as coverings, which were poor protection from the cold. As the snow piled up in drifts, they were in danger of the snow caving in on them and smothering them. They also had to deal with the snow falling in and dripping through the poor substitute for a ceiling.

Oct 30-31, 1846, SNOW, Snow, and More Snow

The snow came down heavily on the 30th of October. There was no break in the snowfall on the 31st. The quiet, cold blankets of white gave no indication of what was to come. The men gathered in small groups and then passed the word along to the women and children. "This is a short storm, be ready to go tomorrow," they said.

At Truckey Lake as well as Donner Lake, the Breens, Eddys, Kesebergs, and Dolan discussed how soon they would leave. "Just let there be a break in the snow and we should move on," urged Mr. Breen.

The morning continued with a bone-chilling cold that seeped through the thickest layers of clothing. Margaret felt the cold as she collected wood for the fire. The cold reached down and seemed to snatch at her heart. She gasped as she imagined icy fingers clutching her beating heart. This was not a normal snow. It began to snow on the Truckey. It had been snowing off and on, but this was a thick, blinding snow. The wind seemed harsher, the air damper and colder. It was a formidable snow storm.

As it snowed, the delay filled George and Tamsen Donner with dread. They had a broken axle with no way to repair it. George's hand had a severe deep cut. Being six miles behind the others, there would be no catching up, and there was no way for the others to know of the trouble they were in. They looked about Alder Creek and considered lying in, just a bit longer, until this white-out ceased. So they made camp planning to move out on foot as soon as possible.

The days began to pass with increasing similarity. The snow was not letting up and blanket upon blanket was stacking up of it.

October 30 and 31, 1846, The Beginning of the Big Snow

By the end of these two days, the Breens and those with them have reached what will be known as Donner Lake. They tried to reach the pass but encountered a wall of snow. They decided to stay by the lake and try again the next day. The Reeds and the others caught up with the Breens. They did not realize that the beginning of the California storm would keep them hostage for the next several months, half a year for some of the survivors. Every day for the next four days, small groups attempted to hike out over the Pass. Each day, they were turned back by the raging, swirling snow. The skies were dark and trying to leave became harder and harder until after the fourth day, they realized, these poor unfortunate emigrants were going to be snowbound for a while.

November 12, the First Attempt to Leave

The first group of fifteen attempted to walk out of the Donner Lake area after several days of waiting. The weather had finally lifted and they believed this would be their chance to walk to Sacramento. They left on foot and were making some progress in the beginning. As they climbed the hills though, the amount of snow was immeasurable and they began sinking as they walked.

Thinking back, William Eddy remembered what an emotional good-bye it was for them. There was crying and weeping and promises to send back a rescue party as soon as they reach Sutter's Fort. He could feel his heart clutch as he thought of his wife and small children. He was sure he could make the trek to Sacramento and bring back relief. As they trudged up the hill, laboring with each snow sucking step, each person was occupied with their own private thoughts wondering if they were ever going to see any of their family again. Each member had a small piece of beef for sustenance—for the whole trip. By the time they reached the top of the Pass, only about three miles, they found themselves sinking back into the snow. The snowbanks were about ten feet deep; the walking had become such a difficult, arduous task. The group was quickly losing their strength and motivation. Sinking almost to the waist as they plunged each leg forward, they realized that without snow shoes, they were doomed. As the sun disappeared and they were enveloped in the dark, the decision was made to walk back. It wasn't until midnight that the fifteen struggled back to the cabins on the Truckee. William Eddy mused that he never thought he'd be happy to see their miserable lean-tos, but he was.

November 13, the Bear

The next day, William Eddy was able to shoot some ducks. Sharing the guns, ammunition, and food, the ducks were quickly devoured. The next day, Mr. Eddy was out hunting again—he noticed bear tracks. By the size of the tracks, he figured it was a Grizzly Bear. Although quite faint from hunger and still tired from the midnight hike the night before, he bravely went after the bear. In other circumstances, he would have gone back for another hunter because the Grizzly are dangerous creatures and even the Indians avoided hunting them.

They are much larger and meaner than black bears and difficult to shoot and kill. He felt if he went back to get another hunter, he would lose the track, and the bear. He wasn't willing to do that. He began to follow his trail. As he stalked the creature through the woods, he came upon the beast. It was foraging in the snow digging roots from the ground. Very quietly, William checked that his gun was loaded and then put an extra bullet in his mouth between his teeth. He knew that once the bear saw him, he would probably charge him and the closer the bullet was to being loaded would improve his chances to live. He pulled the trigger and with the first shot, the bear saw him, or smelled him, and raised up on his two hind feet. He then charged. Eddy got off a second shot and then ran around a tree. Being smaller and quicker, he came up behind the bear and shot him in the shoulder. The bear was slowing down and then dropped. He was still alive but disabled and at that point, William used his gun as a club and smashed the bear's skull. He would find that one bullet pierced the heart and one shot went through the shoulder of the bear. Because of the huge size of the beast, Eddy had to go back to camp to get help with bringing back this prize. Mr. Graves helped him.

It was estimated that the bear weighed 800 pounds. That would provide a lot of food for this starving group. William gave Mr. Foster half of the meat from the bear because it was Mr. Foster's gun that he used. More meat was given to Margaret Reed and Mr. Graves. Many families feasted on fresh meat that night.

The next day, Mr. Eddy was out hunting again and he killed a duck and a grey squirrel. But for the next six days, he couldn't find anything to hunt, and the specter of starvation was again looming over the poor unfortunate souls.

November 29, Donner Lake

It continued to snow and it was very cold. One day, Patty and Tommy were outside the cabin collecting snow to melt: for drinking, cooking, and bathing. They watched Mr. Breen sorrowfully talking to his last surviving oxen, a beast so weak that it stood swaying, its ribs showing clearly through the mottled, rough coat. They watched woodenly as he put his hand on the beast's forehead and quickly slaughtered that last oxen. He hefted one of the huge wooden yokes and walked next door to give another family a little more wood so they could burn it. "There is so little wood around here," he complained. "I don't know what we'll do when we have burned everything. I hope it doesn't keep snowing." He was shaking his head and nodded to Patty and Tommy and then, went back into his chore of skinning and portioning out the meat of his last beast of burden.

December, Donner Lake

They were so hungry. When it wasn't snowing, they walked along the banks of the lake. They could see fish swimming under the thick layer of ice, but they had no way to catch the fish.

December 1846, Plans to Escape

William Eddy went out to hunt every day hoping to supplement his family's meager rations. He caught an owl and a coyote. Although they provided some sustenance, they were small and didn't last long. Every day he went out, he hoped to find larger game. Meanwhile, another group of the wayward pioneers was thinking of a way to get out.

Sitting by the fire in the Graves cabin, the small group talked about walking out of their encampment and finding their way to Sacramento. They realized that someone among them would need to mount a survivor's hike out of the valley to get help and bring them back to those remaining if the others were to survive. This was the beginning of the Forlorn Hope as they would be called.

"The snow is here to stay," said Mr. Graves. "For the next company to walk out of here, we need to make snowshoes to walk on top of the snow and not sink in." They all nodded in agreement with his declarations. The first group tried to walk out of camp in the snow, over the mountains, and they turned back because they had become mired in the snow. Each step they took, they found themselves sinking deeper and deeper into it, sometimes up to their waists. They made little progress forward. To the group's utter frustration, the heavy, wet, waist deep snow forced them to turn back. Because of this failure and with the help of Stanton and the others, Mr. Graves was making several pairs of snowshoes. This time when they tried their trek out of the valley, they succeeded. They could walk on top of the snow.

They were in luck. The snow hadn't fallen for three days. The sun was shining, and the nights were clear, the stars twinkling brightly. With no cloud cover to keep the warmth reflected by the earth, the temperature plummeted. The snow that covered the ground, at least by seven feet by Mr. Graves's estimation, had frozen. Mr. Stanton and Mr. Graves completed making snowshoes, and they were thinking that the next attempt at an escape might be successful. Now, they needed to determine when they would leave.

While the group was plotting their escape, Eliza was contending with Bayliss and his illness. She barely slept at night. She tried to stay awake in case he cried out for her. She was worried about him as he was becoming weaker and weaker. He wasn't eating anymore and she tried to get him to take spoonfuls of melted snow. By now, he wouldn't take anything by mouth and his breathing was ragged. Patty was making a practice of warming skins by the fire and then bringing them to lay over him. His skin was very cool to the touch and he did not open his eyes to any of the activity around him. He seemed not to know where he was or be able to feel any discomfort. Eliza and Patty knew he would not live much longer.

December 13, Alder Creek

Jacob Donner and three other young men, Sam, James, and Joseph, were so weak and ill with fever that their days were numbered. Eliza wrote how lively and fun the three men were in camp on the plains before the snow. The toll of the snow, the unrelenting cold, the continuous storms, the lack of decent shelter, and no food had broken their spirits. She watched them slowly give up. They became depressed and that hastened their death. George Donner was still contending with an infected wound. He also experienced fever and weakness.

Tamsen was on the brink of total exhaustion. Caring for these men in snow soaked tents and brush lean-tos, she expended much of her energy. She had her children to keep alive too. Each day was a trial. What would they do? Twenty-seven people were scratching at survival. She wasn't sure if any of them would live.

December 15, 1846, Donner Lake Camp

Bayliss Williams died. They buried him deep in the snow and covered his burial site with rocks. The hope was that the heavy rocks would keep the animals from digging up his body. The death of Bayliss Williams galvanized the snowshoe company. They could stay and slowly die of starvation or freezing, or they could leave. They decided to leave the next day.

They sent a runner to the Donners at the Alder Creek camp. They had never gotten the axle fixed, so the Donners remained six miles behind the rest of the group. The message was that a group was planning to hike to Sacramento if anyone wanted to join them. Unfortunately, the Donners were dealing with injuries and sickness and no one could leave to join the group. Tamsen wished them success and good fortune in their escape. With a shudder, she turned back to her George, the children, and the others. With a heavy heart, she wished them God speed. *Please, please, hurry back*, she prayed.

December 16, The Forlorn Hope

William Eddy and Mary Ann Graves joined the group of seventeen to become the Forlorn Hope. Each person had dried meat for six days. Six days was the estimated time they would need to climb over the mountain pass and descend into the Sacramento Valley. Surely, there would be no snow and downhill the going would be much easier. The dried meat was the width of two fingers and each hiker would have enough meat for three meals a day. They also had sugar and coffee, which would give them warm liquids to drink by the fire in the mornings and evenings.

The group left in the afternoon on a somewhat sunny day. Fourteen of the group had snowshoes; three of the hikers did not. Patrick Dolan joined the group with Mr. Stanton and Willie Graves. Patrick Dolan told the Reed family that his going would result in one less mouth to feed, and he wanted to help bring the rescue party back.

By the second day, the weather was cloudy but still not snowing, and the group had reached Donner Summit. The snowshoes proved to be a boon for the group. Sadly, two of the hikers, who did not have snowshoes, had to turn back. They sunk up to armpits and could not make any distance at all. The third hiker, without snowshoes, was a 12-year-old Lemule Murphy. Amazingly, he persevered and kept up with the group. Dragging themselves to the top of the ridge, they could see for miles. However, what they saw staggered even the strongest among them. Disappointed, they saw snow that reached deep into the Sacramento Valley.

"Lord almighty, there's nothing but more snow!" lamented Lemule.

However, Mary Graves saw a mist over the valley. "I am sure that is smoke!" she exclaimed. "There must be people down there." She was so insistent that one of the members fired a shot into the valley hoping someone would hear them. No one did. Glumly, she turned back to the group. She tried to say something but was so tired she put her arm around Lemule and they sank down onto the blankets.

When they made camp the third night, they made the fire high and hoped that the last straggler, Charlie Stanton, would catch up to them. Charles Stanton was their guide and knew the trail. Good old Charlie who had already hiked down to the Sacramento Valley once and had come back with provisions for everyone at the Donner Lake encampment had lagged far behind. They were concerned about him.

Mary Graves kept a vigil out for him and when she finally did see him come limping slowly into camp, she went to help him to the fire. She gave him warm coffee sweetened with sugar. He tried to wave it away, but Mary would not let him.

The next morning, it had been five days since their departure. The sky was cloudy, but they made more progress, and although going down hill, the snow was still deep and treacherous. Sometimes icy, it caused walkers to slide and fall. The hard ice-snow having no give as they fell, so it felt like they were falling on concrete. Sometimes there would be a snowdrift, and the heavy snow clung to their layers of clothes, slowly saturating them and becoming heavier as they trudged on. They kept walking, coming nearer to the valley, but nowhere did they see any green fields.

That night, Mary watched again for Charlie. He was taking longer and longer to join the group.

The morning of December 21, the sky opened up and it stormed. By then, Charles Stanton was snow blind. He sat, not seeing, listening to the group talk. This would be their sixth night and they weren't near their goal.

"Are you coming, Charlie?" Mary Graves had wanted to know.

"Yes, I am coming. I will be right behind you." However, he did not move. He made no effort to get up.

Mary threw all the remaining wood on the fire, stoking it, to keep him as warm as possible. She knew in her heart that Charles Stanton, aged thirty-five, who was not married and had no family in the Donner-Reed party, would not be coming. He died sitting by the cold fire pit. A later rescue party would find him frozen by the fire ring. Charles T. Stanton gave his life for the Donner-Reed pioneers. Having no family and no tie to the group, Charlie left the security of Sutter's Fort nonetheless to return with provisions for the unfortunate group. He again volunteered to show the Forlorn Hope the way to the Sacramento Valley. Without him, the group never would have made it to Sutter's Fort.

December 24, Donner Lake

Patty, Tommy, and Jimmy lay on their stomachs in front of the fire. They sliced off strips of the hide they were sitting on and toasted them in the flames. Then they chewed the smoky treats until they were gelatinous mulch in their mouths and swallowed them albeit with much difficulty. At first, Patty wouldn't let the boys toast their own slices. However, they were careful; it became easier for her to watch them toasting the shreds–they did not burn their fingers.

Virginia, Patty, Tommy, and Jimmy were sitting by the fire.

"It's Christmas Eve," declared Patty.

"Do you think that Santa Claus knows where we are?" asked Tommy.

"I don't think he'll be able to find us here in the mountains in the snow," sighed Patty.

"I wish that if he had a present for me, he would give it to Pa," Virginia put in earnestly.

"Oh, do you think he would? He can have my present too. Oh I hope he's…" she trailed off.

"You hope he's what?" Jimmy questioned, puzzled. "Where is he, Virginia?"

"I don't know. I hope he is all right. The last we heard he had been at Sutter's Fort."

"Yes, it has been so long since we heard from him. Now that we aren't walking along the trail, we don't hear from him anymore," Patty said. She wanted to say that she had missed his notes that he used to leave for them, but it had been a while since they had spotted any sign of him. Even knowing he had been safe, she didn't know where he was or how he was now. She looked at Virginia and saw she had turned her head to hide a tear.

"I know he is fine," she declared and hugged Virginia. "Who wants to help me make a pot of glue?" she asked. The pot of glue was what they called the boiled hide stew they made. Everyday, they toasted hide. It was time they made some hide stew. Their clothes hung on them; they were slowly starving to death.

Margaret watched and listened to her children. They were so brave. When they talked of their father, her hand flew to her heart. Her sweet children were going to offer their long missing father their presents. Margaret then smiled a secret smile. She had a Christmas surprise for her innocents. Tomorrow, they would have a Christmas feast and for one day, they would not be starving.

December 25, Christmas Day

It was snowing the entire time on Christmas eve and did not cease even on the day of.

The children were up early, excited because of the day.

Margaret gathered them around and they talked about what they were thankful for and said their prayers. She then left her children to talk and laugh by the fireplace. She had a Christmas dinner to prepare. What to do first? Now was the time to ferret out her secret stores. Wouldn't they be so surprised? She had hidden a teacup full of white beans. There was half that amount of rice. When the last ox was killed, most of the meat had been frozen and kept inside and they had sliced off pieces to cook. The tripe she had carefully cleaned and hung over a part of the cabin–it was soon covered in snow and frozen. Now, it would be part of their dinner.

'I'll be back in a moment," she sang out to the chattering children. She donned her mittens, shawl, and boots. Outside, she unburied her frozen treasure. She also had secured away a small block of bacon. *Oh, what a feast I shall prepare for them today.* She laughed and hugged her skinny self and with excitement and came back into the cabin, not garnering much curiosity from the group. She put the heavy hunk of tripe in a pan with the block of bacon beside it and left them to thaw.

Still smiling, she then dug around in her hiding places and produced a teacup full of dried apples. She started humming and then singing as she lined up the contents for her feast.

Patty got up from the fire surprised and happy her mother was singing, and then she gasped as she saw the food before her. "Oh Ma!" she exclaimed.

Margaret put her finger up to her lips, but it was too late. The others had heard her.

Virginia, followed by the boys, jumped up. "What is it?" she asked in response to Patty's exclamation.

"Oh look!" cried Patty as she grasped both of Virginia's hands and they twirled around.

"Me, me!" shouted Tommy and Jimmy laughed.

"Oh, Mother, what have you here?" Virginia cried out.

"I have a Christmas feast to serve you tonight. Tonight, you shall have all you want to eat. We shall eat until our tummies burst."

"Such a wonderful idea," said Virginia dreamily.

"I can't wait for supper. When will supper be?" demanded Jimmy.

"I want to eat, I want to eat!" Tommy was jumping up and down.

"All in due time, dear ones." Margaret made a production of finding the right pans for her cooking. "I hope we will have enough wood." She smiled at them knowing she had a small pile that she saved along with the other treats. "Now the meat is thawing, let's hear some Christmas carols."

They sang as they sat by fire. Each child was trying to contain their excitement and dreaming of the fabulous meal to come.

Later, they danced around the fire as they watched the bacon sizzle and crisp in the pan. They sniffed at the air hungrily. Each could feel the cramping in their stomachs. What a delicious concoction of smells filled the small room, what paradise! Then, Margaret added water and the tripe. She added the cup of beans and they all watched and waited for the mixture to boil. The cabin filled with the delicious smell of the cooking meats. Every time a white bean floated to the top, they cheered and danced about the fire, singing and laughing, and every once in a while, a tear streaked down a child's sallow cheek.

Near the end of her preparation, Margaret put the apples in the water. The delicate, sweet fragrance of apples added another layer to the wonderful smells in the cabin. Hugging, kissing, laughing, as well as dancing, and a few tears were the emotions that washed in waves over the Reed family. Eliza had joined in the frivolity. Her sadness at the death of her brother, Bayliss, secreted in her heart was put aside for the moment of joy.

As they sat down to their Christmas dinner, Margaret clasped her hands and looked at each child. "You shall have as much as you want to eat," she promised as she dished up the fragrant spoonfuls. "Eat slowly. But enjoy this wondrous bounty."

After grace, they started eating slowly, and it was very quiet in the cabin. As they enjoyed each mouthful and became more sated, the laughter and chatter resumed. Soon, the noise level was as loud as when they were dancing and watching the banquet being prepared.

"What a lovely Christmas it was!" Patty said as she hugged her mother.

"All of our food was so delicious," agreed Virginia. "I am so stuffed, so warm, and happy, I won't want to eat again."

Margaret smiled, but inside, her heart clenched. Tomorrow, they would be hungry again. She looked out the window and it was still snowing. She wondered if this would be their last true meal, ever. She sighed and looked down.

"Ma, Ma!" Tommy was tugging at her skirt. She smiled, bent down, picked him up, and then went to sit by the fire. She gently rocked him to sleep. The other children sat around the fire with her. Each was thinking their private thoughts about their wonderful Christmas and not being hungry.

December 25, Alder Creek

Tamsen Donner had hoped for another day of sun. Even a cloudy day without snow would have been so welcome. Nevertheless, by mid-afternoon, it was snowing again. Heavy, wet snow quickly built up on their tents. They had to leave the shelter of the tents to rake the snow off the canvas to keep it from crushing their humble abodes and crashing to the ground. For the Donners who were ill and weak, the effort was sapping their strength.

She wondered if Virginia was still reading *The Life of Daniel Boone.* She smiled as she remembered how excited the girl was to receive the book and had read it several times wearing out the cover. By now, it had surely been used for fodder for the fire. Now, it was only a memory in the child's mind.

December 25, Forlorn Hope

The snowstorm pelted the rag-tag Forlorn Hope. There were only eleven of them left alive. Franklin Graves knew he was dying. He called his youngest daughter to him.

"You must promise me these things," he said. "When you marry, and you will, you must always cherish your husband as he will cherish you. You must also promise me to revolt at nothing that will keep you alive. You must promise, I know you will keep your promise." She did promise.

Franklin Graves knew he was dying, and he knew how to keep his children alive. By forcing them to agree in a deathbed promise, a promise they had to keep, he had assured their survival.

That night, the eleven shivering bodies huddled under blankets. William Eddy did his best to keep the group together trying to keep them warm. He continually rubbed his hands together and encouraged the others to do the same. The snow was so wet and heavy, they could not build a fire. The miserable bunch crowded together quaking with a bone numbing coldness. They tried to meld as one, rubbing their hands as William had shown them. Mary and Harriet were so cold, tired, and miserable that they mindlessly followed the instructions. They took turns pushing up with their arms against the blanket to keep the snow from piling up above and smothering them.

Stranded on that mountainside, with three dead ones, they now gave themselves a new name: Camp Death. It was day ten.

December 27, Camp Death

The miserable eleven crowded together for warmth. Fitful sleep interrupted by dreams of food and arm pain, as more than one survivor could relate, waking up to someone trying to bite into their arm was the unattainable goal.

That day was the first time that they ate the flesh of one of their dead. Three bodies who were: Antonio, Patrick Dolan, and Franklin Graves. There was no wood to collect for the fire. The group had their blankets mounded under a pine tree. As the starving group tried to start a fire, there was a mishap. William Eddy tried to start it under the blankets of their nest with his powder horn. It backfired and he was severely burned. They packed his injured, burned arms in the snow. Then Harriet Pike offered material from her coat. As the clouds parted, they were able to start a fire. Since there was no wood, they set fire to the pine tree that they sat under. The burning boughs, ash, and embers rained down upon them. Then, they sliced the flesh from Patrick Dolan's body. No one could look at another as they ate their meal in shame and tears.

Lemule was delirious and refused all food and drink. He would die that night.

The next three days, they sought refuge under the blankets. Each felt that they could soon die as well. Eating the frozen flesh was one way to continue living. They felt sorrow, but now, the intense horror of before had lessened.

Mary remembered her father's words. She said small prayers to him as she choked down her meals.

December 30, 1846, Camp Death

Finally, a morning when the sky was grey, but the snow had let up. They were on the move again. Now, they numbered ten: five women and five men. Everyone had a pair of snowshoes. They had two Indian guides with them. They were the ones to carve up the meat from the bodies and to pack it up and take the bundles along with them.

Moving west, they spent the next two days winding through canyon country.

One of their men in the back of the pack, Jay Fosdick, was growing weaker. All those of the original Forlorn Hope were wondering how much farther they had left? What would happen if they ran out of what little food they have? What happened to the supposed six nights duration for this trip? It has taken them fifteen days and they still weren't there yet.

New Year's Day, 1847

It has snowed lightly through the night. Patrick Breen had been sure there was going to be a huge snow storm, but only light snow was falling. The skies were grey and it was cold and windy. They were stranded in their cabins. The snow was so deep they saw tree tops. They couldn't cut these for firewood. Because of the deep snow, they sank when they tried to walk out. It was so quiet not even a bird could be heard chirping, and there is virtually no game for hunting.

"Donner Lake is thick with ice. There is no hope of fishing and no animals come to the lake to drink. We are in dire need of a miracle," Patrick wrote in his diary. He wrote everyday, even if it was only to document a weather report. He prayed and read the Bible passages to comfort those who came to listen.

The only food they had to eat were ox hides. The hides offer no nutrition, but when chewed into a gelatinous pulp, they give the stomach some feeling of satiety. "At least you can sleep with the feeling of something in your stomach," Mr. Breen had said.

January 4, 1847, Donner Lake

The snow continued to fall, the white walls around them slowly growing higher.

January 4 began as a sunny day. This was the day they would try their escape. Margaret, after much soul searching, realized she had to do something to try and save her family. Eliza, Virginia, and Milt Elliot had decided today would be the day they would begin the hike out over the mountains. After all, the first group had gone, but no one had returned. It had been twenty days since they left. It was supposed to take six nights and seven days to reach Sutter's Fort. They surmised something had happened to all fifteen. Now was the time. Something had to be done. Everyone here was dying.

Margaret had debated at great length if she would go and who she would go with. She couldn't take the smaller children and someone would need to stay with them. Patty was the logical choice.

Patty had understood that she and her mother and Virginia would be separated. However, Patty knew she would have to be brave and take care of Jimmy and Tommy and wait for her mother's return.

The tears cascaded down her cheeks; she kept sniffing and swiping at her face to dispel the tears. Jimmy and Tommy stood at her side. They had walked part way, to say goodbye. Patty wanted to watch her mother and Virginia for as long as possible. When they were out of sight, she slowly patted the boys and they trooped back to the very quiet and seemingly colder cabin.

January 4, Camp Death

Mary and Harriet sat listlessly trying to gather their strength to start again. Even downhill, the walk was agonizing. As Mary stood, she noticed blood coming from her worn shoes. Ignoring it, she put on her snowshoes. Both she and Harriet had feet with black toes—the result of frostbite. *One nice thing about frostbite, she thought idly, the toes don't hurt.* She knew everyone suffered from frostbite. They viewed their black toes, fingers, and bleeding feet clinically, each wondering who would be the next to fall and die.

Their cache of human flesh was gone. Jay Fosdick would be the next to die. He was snow blind and lagged far behind the group. That night, when making camp in only three feet of snow, Jay lumbered into camp and collapsed but was still breathing. The group made plans for leaving the next morning wondering if he would make it.

That evening, as they crowded together, toasting strips of hide from their snowshoes, William Foster proposed an idea. "We may only make it through tomorrow without food. This rawhide is not nourishment. We should kill Luis and Salvadore. They are only Indians."

"We can't kill our guides!" protested William Eddy.

"It is Luis who has gotten us lost," countered Foster.

"Only because he couldn't see the landmarks he knows. The snow has been too deep."

"They are Indians. They are different from us. I think they would gladly give their lives for us," replied Foster stubbornly.

The argument continued for a short time. The suggestion to draw lots for who is next to die was voted down in favor of sacrificing the Christian Miwoks. The verdict: The Indians should die.

William Eddy felt strongly that this was wrong. These Indians had risked their lives to guide this group to Sutter's Fort. Feeling strongly that this would be wrong, Eddy approached Luis and told him of the plan. Both Luis and Salvadore slipped away, and now they numbered eight: five women and three men.

The next morning, after disappointment and suspicions that Eddy had told the Indians of their plan, the group strapped on their snowshoes, all the worst for wear. Mary Graves and Eddy, the strongest of the eight, planned to go ahead. William Eddy took his rifle in hopes of flushing out game because they were still starving and if they did not eat, they would all die.

Ironically, they knew which way to go. They followed the trail of Luis and Salvadore.

January 5, 1847, Donner Camp

The sun was shining that day. After much planning and a long tearful goodbye, Margaret and Virginia Reed, Milt Elliot and Eliza Williams began their quest to Sutter's Fort.

Patty looked at her mother with a tear stained face. "I will take care of Jimmy and Tommy, Ma. The Breens are good people, we will be fine."

The small group staggered out to begin their climb over Donner Summit.

Camp Death

Finally, below the snow line, William Eddy and Mary Ann Graves went downhill. They saw a crushed grass area, and presuming that deer had slept there, they started looking in earnest for them. They heard some sudden movement and noticed a doe. Eddy fired, but the doe ran off.

"You've missed it," cried Mary Ann dejectedly. They slowly moved to where the doe ran. "But wait, I see blood!" she said excitedly.

The two energized by possible success and tracked it down. It lay on the ground. Eddy slit its throat, and they built a fire to roast the deer. As they nodded off to sleep, they hoped the rest of the Forlorn Hope group had heard the shot and that they would see the fire and know there was food. They fell to sleep not knowing that Jay Fosdick had died.

January 6, 1847, Having to Turn Back

Only two days into their trek, Eliza felt her body and will fading. Try as she might, she couldn't keep up with the small group. She could feel the tears freezing on her face. Her feet felt like they were frozen solid and it took great effort for her to lift them. She longed for Patty, Tommy, and Jimmy back in the warm, although dark and smoky, cabin. Unable to keep up with group, she turned back to walk back to the camp. Margaret thought about protesting, but Eliza looked so miserable and her mouth was set. Margaret knew that her pleading Eliza to keep walking up the mountain with them would not work and kissed her goodbye. She felt a stab of jealousy that Eliza would be returning to her children, her babies, that she might never see again. She could feel her heart breaking and the tears freezing on her cheek. She watched Eliza stagger-stepping, forcing her feet one in front of the other, even if going going downhill the effort for her was gargantuan. Upon reaching her goal and seeing the crude cabin Eliza could only feel desolation and frustration of not being able to leave this awful place. She stifled the urge to scream when she saw the pitiful cabin in front of her. Her hand trembled as she pushed open the door. She was exhausted and could not go any further. She collapsed into Patty's arms so upset that she couldn't leave the Camp of Death.

Although upset that she hadn't made it, Patty was thrilled to see Eliza. She felt disappointment that her mother hadn't returned but happy that she was on her way to freedom.

"Oh Eliza, don't despair." Patty was smoothing Eliza's hair as it rested on her shoulder. "I am sure glad you are here! I'm sorry you didn't make it out, but we are very happy to see you."

Jimmy and Tommy crowded around her, and the four sat together in silence. Patty stoked the fire and melted snow to give Eliza a warming drink. She put a blanket around her and slowly stroked her hair murmuring that they were glad she was back. "There would be other times to escape," Patty had comforted the bedraggled Eliza, "and maybe we will be able to climb out with you." She looked at the one set of snowshoes they were all supposed to use. Their time to be rescued would be coming and soon, she hoped, before they all died.

The next day brought a few swirls of snow, and the fact that it wasn't snowing hard brought Patty some comfort as she thought of her mother and Virginia. She wondered how far they had gotten and worried about the cold and hardships they were enduring.

January 8, Donner Lake Camp

The next morning, the weather seemed the same. Patty had gotten everyone up and was putting away the meager fixings she had prepared for breakfast. The day seemed as monotonous as the others until she heard some noise outside. Not daring to hope that it might be her mother or rescuers, she waited. She could feel her heart thumping in her chest. Little Cash noticed her excitement and came to sit by her. Then she saw her mother. Oh, the joy she felt! Her heart felt like it was filling up her chest and she almost couldn't breathe. She clapped her hands silently close to her breast. Patty knew she should be sad that her mother had not made it out, but all she felt was joy at seeing her return. With tears coursing down her cheeks, she and Cash ran outside and she flung herself in her mother's arms. Cash danced wildly about their legs yipping with joy.

"We couldn't find out a way up through the mountains," Margaret said bitterly, hugging her daughter. "We kept trying different paths only to be forced to come back. The only food we had to eat was the hides and I became so weak and tired, I just couldn't keep on going. So I came back," she finished as they walked into the cabin. "I left Virginia and came back." She collapsed into bed and didn't even stir when Patty brought her some warmed snow. Patty took a cloth and dipped it into the warmed water and squeezed the liquid into her mother's mouth. She watched her swallow and repeated the gesture. When the water was gone, she laid the warm cloth on her mother's forehead. Soon she was breathing rhythmically asleep and only then did Patty leave her side. Now she wondered how her sister was after five days in the snow on that cold, stormy mountain with no food and without Margeret.

January 8, Persevering

Virginia had suffered frostbite in her toes. They were black and the pain was excruciating as the others tried to warm her toes. It seemed uncertain if Virginia would be able to walk out when the group tried their next escape.

The weather was turning dark and cloudy and by the next day, it was snowing for the next four days. By then, the snow level was higher than the shanty they were living in. Wood was very scarce. Not only were they afraid of starving to death, but now they might freeze as well.

They began to carve foot holds in the snow wall and climb to its top and then being at a higher level, they would cut off tree branches and the tree tops where they could. It was becoming more difficult to find wood. Patty wondered if they would freeze first.

* * * * *

Many years later, a stump by the Graves/Reed cabin was found. The tree had been topped off where the level of the snow was in 1846 and 1847. The top of the stump measured twenty-two feet high. Today, at the Donner summit, there is a memorial to the Donner Party and it measures twenty-two feet high showing the pinnacle of the snow.

January 10, Camp Death

There were seven white survivors in the Forlorn Hope and two Miwok Indians. Luis and Salvadore have been employed by John Sutter to help the settlers find their way back to Sacramento. The group of seven whites had become desperate and vicious in their starvation. The actions of the group, especially those of William Foster, have frightened Luis and Salvadore. They know they have been targeted to die and they slipped away at night. They left a trail of blood from their raw, wounded feet.

The Forlorn Hope continued following the bloody foot trail. The flesh from doe and Jay Fosdick was only a memory now. They were starving. William Foster, weak and muttering, was tracking the footprints like a hunter. He was planning on shooting the Indians when he saw them.

The group came to an abrupt halt by a stream, and there before them, lying in exhaustion, were Luis and Salvadore. Foster raised his rifle and approached the Indians. Eddy, Mary Ann, Amanda, and the two other women turned away as the rifle fired.

January 26, 1847, Donner Lake

Eating the cow and oxen hides that covered the floors gave them no energy, no sustenance, and no calories. There was no food and each day, they got weaker. All of the mules and oxen were gone. Some were thought to be lost in the snow or stolen by the Indians. Margaret knew that in order for her family to stay alive, they had to eat the only source of food that was left. She looked at Little Cash stretched out by the fire with Patty and the boys.

"We have no food," she stated. She walked over to the fire and placed her hand on Cash's head.

Patty looked up at her mother, tears in her eyes, but she knew this to be true. She hugged the dog but sat there as her mother led the dog outside. She heard a dull thump and then she cried.

We had to kill our little dog Cash and eat him. We ate his head and feet and hide and everything about him. Virginia Reed's diary Jan 26, 1847

* * * * *

January 31, 1847

Although with a heavy heart after learning of the murder of his two Indian guides, John Sutter put together a rescue relief party. He outfitted seven men on horseback with pack mules. He was not paid for these efforts. He knew he may never be paid, but his generosity and good nature never wavered. The Forlorn Hope had no money but was assured that those left in Donner Camp had money.

February 3, 1847

James Reed was in Yerba Buena. He went to a public meeting in a saloon. Telling of the plight of those stranded in the sierras, he urged all who were listening to donate money for a relief party. He was able to raise several hundred dollars and with that money, he bought supplies, horses, and mules. While putting together his rescue mission, word came about the survivors of the Forlorn Hope. They were shocked to hear how horrid the conditions were. They shuddered to hear about those left being reduced to eating human flesh. They also knew where the emigrants were now. Some survivors were at the Donner Camp and the others at the Aldrich Creek.

James Reed was anxious to get to his family. He hoped and prayed that they were still alive. He felt no animosity towards those who banned him from the group. He understood the tragedy of Snyder's death. He held no grudges except against Mr. Keseberg who had raised the tongue of his wagon and shouted to the others to hang him.

He left for the Sierra Mountains getting a head start by boarding a schooner, which would leave the group up on the Feather River. This cut off twenty miles of travel.

February 9, Donner Camp

Milton Elliot who was staying at the Murphy cabin died. Virginia and her mother dragged his body out of the cabin.

"He was such a good friend," Virginia commented as they said prayers over his slowly freezing body.

Patrick Breen recorded the death in his diary. He wondered where the Forlorn Hope group was. Had they made it? Would anyone come back and save his family? He prayed to God that not all was in vain, but he had doubts that his prayers were heard out in this frozen and, for all he knew, God forsaken land. What had they done in coming here? He wondered. Had he condemned his family to certain death?

Virginia came to visit him in his cabin and Patrick would pull down his Bible and read to the girl. "She seems to find such comfort when I read to her," he had remarked to his wife. "It is a shame for these children to be living through such hardship. So much death, starvation, and there is nothing I can do to lessen the load." He prayed extra hard that night hoping for some break, some solace to come their way.

Feb 19, 1947, Donner Lake, the Relief Party Arrives

Oh, the excitement that day as the relief party arrived! Seven mules laden with food and provisions slowly approached the Donner camp.

Starving, cold hands reddened with chill blains and fingertips white with pending frostbite frantically helped unload the seven mules. Some of the food was opened and eaten as they were standing and unloading the provisions. Shocked by the horrible state of the survivors, the rescuers exchanged glances and could not believe the way they looked and smelled. They were gaunt, ill, and showed signs of frostbite, and some had coughing fits that rattled and shook their bodies whole. Their shoes were torn and tied with strips of clothes, their wardrobe was tattered, and many wore blankets as shifts and jackets. The survivors did not know how to act with the rescuers; they could see the revulsion on their faces.

The joy of being rescued was mixed with the agony of lost lives and the life they had been living. In no time, the food was consumed. They wanted to eat the mules as well, but John Sutter provided the mules as pack animals only and he wanted them back. They were invaluable animals. However, they would help guide them back to Sutter's Fort. They could help carry the small children. Thus thinking of their escape, they turned their greedy eyes away from the food sources.

Feb 22, Donner Lake, Time to Go

Thirty people left traveling towards the Johnson's Ranch in Sacramento.

"All of the food is gone. There is but one hide left to eat. We have to form another party to trek out over the mountains. Are you willing and ready Mrs. Reed?"

Margaret nodded. She knew in order for her children to survive, they had to leave. It wouldn't stop snowing and to stay at the Starvation camp meant death.

Party left with eighteen individuals including Virginia, Margaret, Patty, and Tommy.

They started bravely enough. Patty held Tommy's hand. Each step was a monumental effort. The continuing snow mounded softly and made each step treacherous. Often, they would sink up to their hips with just one move. Tommy and Patty overheated, and Tommy wanted to take off his coat, but Patty knew he had to wear it. Their legs were soaking wet. Their shoes were wet and heavy. It took so much effort to raise each leg out of the snow and when they stepped down, they usually sank back to their hips or their waist. Tommy was crying and whimpering. Patty had tears coursing down her cheeks. They couldn't do this.

The group came to a halt. Margaret held her hand to her face and bit her finger to keep from screaming. Tommy and Patty were exhausted. No one in the group could carry them and they couldn't go any further.

Two men, Moultry and Glover, volunteered to take the two children back.

They had said that they were Masons. Patty knew her father was a Mason and that the men considered themselves a brotherhood.

Patty asked the men if they were truly Masons. They concurred.

"Do you promise on your honor as a Mason that you will take my children back to the camp safely?" Margaret had implored. She gave them a watch as partial payment promising more later.

They promised they would. One more time, Margaret had to rely on strangers to help her. She offered money to the men when they all met in Sacramento. Whether she would see them or her two children again, she did not know.

What she did know was that if she and her other daughter didn't make it to Sacramento, they would die. What could she do? She had buried her son before they left Illinois. She had buried her mother on the trail. Now, if she didn't continue, her son Jimmy and daughter Virginia and her would die. However, if she did go on, she had turned her back on her dear Patty and Tommy.

"Goodbye mother," Patty said, "if we are meant to see each other again, we will. We must do what we have to for now." They kissed and embraced each other furiously. Then the two groups said goodbye.

Patty and Tommy returned to the Donner camp with Moultry and Glover, who returned them safely.

Back at the Donner camp, the men brought the children to the Breens cabin. Mr. Breen looked down at the totally spent children. He, who had seven mouths to feed and did not have any extra resources, agreed to take the children in.

Feb 22, Alder Creek

The need for food outweighed the fear, the repugnance, and the moral objections to eating human flesh. They knew where the bodies were buried. They needed to find them to live.

Feb 23, Donner Lake

The desperation of these pioneers has never been so severe. Knowing that the Donners at the Alder Creek have said they will eat available flesh, Mr. Breen has now come to the conclusion that they must do something. They must survive.

Back at the Breen/Reed cabin, Mr. Breen took his faithful friend Towser outside. He knelt by the dog. "You have been a loyal friend. Now, you are giving us your last gift, the gift of life." He wiped a tear from his cheek. The dog looked soulfully into his eyes and licked him one last time. He put the gun to the dog's head and said mournfully, "I'm sorry, friend." He cried as he shot him in the head. This was the last dog in the camp. He would now be food for his children and his extensive family.

Elizabeth Graves heard the shot. She stiffened and quickly thought about who was shot. It could only mean food. She wound a scarf around her head, pausing for a moment to reflect on what she had become. Here, she was reduced to begging for food. Everything was gone now, and she had nothing with which to bargain. She had to go to another and beg like a dog. She shook her head, put on her gloves, and, squaring her shoulders, went over to the Breen cabin.

"Please Mr. Breen, we have no food. Could you spare something?"

Mr. Breen shook his head. "I now have nine mouths to feed, dear one. I cannot spare any food. I'm sorry my child." His lips quivered and as she left, head bowed, raised his head to the heavens. "Dear Lord, we are so hungry. Will you not answer our prayers?"

He wondered what they had done to anger God so much. Were they all destined to die?

Feb 24, on the Ascent, Trekking Out

On the trail, John Denton was on his last legs. He staggered to sit by the fire and sank down. He sat close to it and then was motionless for a while. He refused dinner and in the morning, asked them to stoke up the fire. He sat there looking warm, comfortable, and even though they knew he was going to sit there and die, everyone in the group wanted to stay with him. They envied his last stand, so to speak.

Jimmy sat down next to John. "I want to stay here with you by the fire. I don't want to walk any more. Please let me stay, Ma."

Distressed, Margaret hurried over to him. "No, you must come with us. Mr. Denton is waiting for the next group to come by. You can't stay here. You must come with me."

"No!" cried Jimmy. "I'll stay."

John Denton sat and didn't have the energy to say yay or nay. He watched the desperate mother and her equally desperate child argue and try to come to terms with what he wanted. Jimmy was so tired and all he wanted to do was sit and wait. He wasn't sure what he would be waiting for, but he could not fathom walking any further in the wet snow. Margaret felt an ache that welled up in her chest. The fear that Jimmy would stay there and die with John gripped her; she could feel herself shaking and it was not from the cold. She felt herself getting hysterical. Taking some deep breaths to calm herself, she smoothed her dress and, with shaking hands, she gently held onto Jimmy's shoulders and turned him towards her.

"I will not be able to bear it if you do not come with me," she said softly. She looked intently into her son's eyes. She stood up and held her hand out.

With a few weaker, crying protestations, Jimmy slowly got up, kissed John Denton on the cheek, took his mother's hand, and slowly walked away. Everyone in the group kept looking behind them hoping that he would get up and start walking after them. With each step they took away from the campfire, the reality set in that he was not going to budge. They watched as the hunched, sitting figure of John Denton became more obscure. A rescue group would find him sitting just so when they came through in the late spring.

Feb 25, 1847, Donner Lake

The tenuous life of those remaining at the Donner Lake encampment continued.

The group barely talked or even looked at one another. So haggard and poorly each felt, it was all they could do to manage to chew on the remaining hides and melt some snow to drink. Although there was some flesh to eat—human flesh—it still took an overwhelming need to live and to eat the meat that was there.

February 26, Alder Creek

The Donner survivors were starving. Having much less than the nothing the traveling companions had at Donner Lake, their life was even more tenuous and danger even more imminent than their friends' condition. They were slowly dying.

Digging where he remembered they had buried some bodies, Jean Baptiste Trudeau was trying to uncover some frozen flesh. Knowing if he could find some food, he could feed himself and the others.

Donner Lake Camp

At Donner Lake, Patty Reed, who had turned nine years old, was suffering from a toothache. *Funny*, Patty had thought to herself. *We are starved to death and I feel sorry for myself because my tooth hurts. I probably could not eat even if I were given meat.* M r s . Murphy, knowing Milt Elliott had died on February 9, was digging through the snow to find his body.

March 1 through March 3, Donner Lake

What joy! James Reed arrived to find his daughter, Patty, sitting on the cabin roof, feet brushing the snow. His son Tommy was also safe thanks to the generosity and kindness of the Breens. The plan was to leave in a few days to the safety and snowless land of Sacramento. Mr. Breen was told the snow will stay on the ground until June. "If the weather is clear, we must leave." Mr. Breen was hesitant. His concern lay with the trek out. *Can they make the long, arduous walk in their debilitated condition*, he wondered. Mr. Breen excused himself to go into the other room and pray. Praying has kept him sane and has given him strength during these long, lonely, dark months.

The Reed party was composed of ten men with many provisions. They quickly distributed the food to all of the remaining families.

The survivors were dirty, tattered, upright skeletons. Their living conditions were utterly deplorable. James Reed bathed his children and helped the Breen family clean up as well. Scouting around the cabin with the snow at the roofline, he found his old friend and employee, Milt Elliott. His body, severely mutilated, was used as necessary food source. James gazed at Milt. "I am so sorry it ended this way. Thanks for standing by my family when I was sent away. You were a true friend." He said a prayer over his friend and then took him outside for a proper burial. Several of the men who had accompanied him on the rescue mission were also burying the dead.

Exploring the shabby hovels that had been used for homes, James scouted out the remaining people in the Donner Lake area. He came upon Lewis Keseberg–the man who wanted to lynch James Reed when Reed and Snyder had their altercation. Mr. Reed helped the man bathe himself and made sure he had enough food to eat. He cleaned out the waste in his cabin and made sure he was comfortable and knew of the plans to leave soon. Years later, in his memoirs, Mr. Keseberg admitted to feeling so guilty for the way he mistreated James Reed, the man he wanted to murder.

March 3, Donner Lake, Time to Leave

The second party of twenty-two emaciated pioneers left for the long trek to Sutter's Fort. James Reed along with eight men from the relief party from Sutter's Fort were leading the way. Two men stayed behind to help the five survivors who remained at the Alder Camp and the Donner Lake sites. Tamsen and George Donner stayed at the Alder camp. George has become very feeble and ill. He too was too ill to leave and Tamsen would not leave him. Lewis Keseberg was still at the Donner Lake camp.

March 5, 1847, the Trip Out

Again, the snow was blanketing the ground. All of the provisions were gone and again they were stranded in a windy snow and ice storm. A foot of snow fell all through the night and the men who were chaperoning them south worked hard to keep the fires going throughout the night. The next morning, they could not see more than several feet in front of them.

The next day, as the storm continued to rage, Isaac Donner who was only five years of age did not wake up. Patty Reed and Mary Donner had slept with him between them, but they could not keep him from death.

They were stuck there for one more freezing day and night.

At the Alder Creek, they were waiting for another rescue party. Margaret Breen became hysterical and was afraid her children would die in this snow bound rescue camp. She blamed James Reed for their deaths. James Reed could only sympathize with her; he has lost his vision to snow blindness and could only sit and wait for rescue himself. Towards midday, his sight returned and he continued to move ahead with Patty, Tommy, and the others.

By the end of the day, they have had to make a huge fire on a platform, which was slowly sinking into the several feet of snow. The group decided to call themselves "Starved Camp."

March 9, 1847, Starved Camp

The next morning, Elizabeth Graves and her son, Franklin, who was only five years old, were found dead. Frozen stiff, they were lying at the edge of the fire pit which has sunk into the snowdrifts.

James Reed and his children have moved on and they camped near what is now known as Kingvale and as they hiked out, the second place they camped is now known as Cisco Grove.

March 12, Second Relief Party

Led by James Reed, the second relief party has reached the Bear Valley. Bear Valley was where the Johnson's Ranch was, and all six members of the Reed family were reunited and they were all safe and alive. Carried all the way from her home, Patty had her "Dolly," a tiny doll, a lock of her grandmother's hair tied with ribbon, and a small pincushion. Although they had been told to bring nothing, Patty had brought these few treasures in her skirt's pocket.

March 14, Donner Camp

The third rescue party reached the Starved Camp. Eleven people have been living in the snow surrounded fire pit since March 6. They have survived by eating the bodies of two children and one adult. The Breens have survived for one week, keeping seven children alive in that frozen pit, four of whom were not their own. When the rescuers arrived, the Breens were near out of their heads with the craziness of trying to stay alive in a snow pit with only dead bodies to nourish themselves.

They heard Tamsen Donner had refused to leave the Alder Creek because her husband and her son Sammy, four years old, were there and unable to travel. On March 21, 1847, Sammy Donner died. Tamsen has been nursing Sammy and her husband George for weeks.

Now, she had one patient. George was slowly dying from gangrene. His arm was injured in the accident when their wagon broke down and was now black and green from his hand to his shoulder. When the accident happened, he joked about his "scratch." He became worried as it did not heal and it slowly progressed to life threatening injury. Tamsen had known for months that this would be a non-healing injury. She remembered back in October when they had tried to make it to the Donner Lake encampment. That was when George had gouged his hand. It had never healed and slowly progressed to this putrid state. Tamsen knew that when the wound grew in size and would not heal that these would be his final days.

March 26, Alder Creek

Tamsen tended to George, but he was getting weaker. He had stopped talking to her and, now, would not sip the warmed, melted snow she tried to force between his cracked lips. She would dip the corner of a rag into a sweetened liquid of melted snow and her last remaining sugar lumps, but even after putting it into his mouth, he no longer suckled the tip of the cloth. "Oh, what am I going to do without my George?" She cried silently into her fists. She prayed for him and for her girls. What a wretched end they had finally come to. All of their plans to start up the Donner family business in the new territory and a school for girls were no longer a possibility. Their dreams scattered on a miserable, sandy trail on the way to a snowy meadow of death. All of their lovely books were gone, destroyed, or left on the trailside. She didn't even know but hoped her girls were still alive. She could not imagine the anguish they must have been experiencing trying to go on. She herself had felt the life draining from her. How was it going to end?

As she looked at George, she realized he had stopped breathing. "Oh George, your suffering is over now," she said softly as she kissed his cheek. She wondered, sitting by her dead husband, how much longer it would be before she died as well.

With indomitable strength, Tamsen Donner set off on her last trek.

She walked the miles to Donner Lake and to Lewis Keseberg. She was hoping to see her children one more time.

Keseberg marveled at the strength of this woman, this mother, who after having her husband die in her arms, walked through the snow with no guide to the Donner camp. She was wet, chilled, and nearly frozen when she arrived at Keseberg's door. She told Lewis about the money she had secreted in her quilt and that it was to be used for her children if she died before she was re-joined by her family. Lewis Keseberg promised he would take the money to her children. However, that promise was never kept.

*   *   *   *   *

March 30, 1847

Tamsen Donner died! Lewis Keseberg was now the lone survivor at the Donner Lake. Tamsen arrived at his door soaking wet and frozen and died by morning regardless of his attempts to warm her and save her life. When the last rescue party arrived at the Donner Lake, Lewis Keseberg was said to be seen eating her corpse—her liver—and had blood on his face. The debate will continue for 150 years about whether Keseberg murdered her or not. Tamsen was considered strong and in good health two weeks before her death. Some question whether she could become so ill and debilitated in two weeks. Keseberg did not help his case by his behavior when the rescuers came or in later years by opening a restaurant and telling people human flesh was the best he had ever eaten.

Those who participated in the rescues were the ones who brought back the stories of the horrors of those stranded in the Sierras. It is human nature to embellish and to err on the side of making a good story better. So one must use good judgment when hearing some of the tales of the Donner party.

April 4, Keseberg Left

Not knowing that Tamsen Donner was dead, the rescue parties talked of rescuing her and Lewis Keseberg. Lewis Keseberg would wait out one last storm before being the final person to be rescued from the Donner/Reed party.

April 16, It Has Been a Year

Believe it or not, it has been one year since the Reed and Donner families began their trek leaving friends and families in Springfield, Illinois, to find their Utopia in the lands of the west.

April 18, 1847, the Final Rescue

Seven more rescuers had arrived to complete the saving of the final survivors of the Donner party. They believed Tamsen Donner and Lewis Keseberg were still alive and pushed forward to the Donner Lake Camp. The snow was easily ten feet deep still making travel difficult and impassable in some places. Sometimes slushy, oftentimes sinking to their waists, it was a difficult trip for them.

This group knew that even if there were no living emigrants remaining, there would be gold and silver and other treasures that were left behind. Some of these riches would be out in the open, others were buried. The hope of the owners was that they would be returning for their possessions. Now, their goods would be plundered.

When they came upon Lewis Keseberg, he told them sadly of Tamsen Donner's death. He also told them that the Donners was a wealthy couple and that Tamsen had told him of the money left behind and that it was to be given to her children.

Lewis Keseberg, thinking of the fortune he was sure that was in the tented shelters the Donners subsisted in, left for the Alder Creek encampment. He was not aware that he was being observed by the

Indians. Washoe Indians would visit the site the next day. They had heard rumors of the crazy white man and they had been afraid of the madness exhibited by those living in the ramshackle lean-tos and cabins. Assured that if they approached when they were still there that they too would become as crazy.

Starved Camp

At the Starved Camp, trekking out to be rescued, Mary Donner, who was only seven years old, fell into a fire and burned her foot badly. A foot that was frozen to begin with and would have to be amputated to save her life.

Articles were appearing in the California Star, which was the newspaper of the area. The name San Francisco was printed on the front-page masthead replacing the name Yerba Buena. Copies sold like hot cakes as everyone was talking about the Donner party and how they had to survive unspeakable tragedy and hardships. A man called Selim E. Woodworth was recounting stories of the rescue he participated in. A midshipman, Woodworth, recounted the rescues of his mission barely mentioning a true heroic rescuer, John Stark, who did the rescue of the Breens family and others all by himself. As the days passed by, many stories of the Donner party were altered. Such wealth of terror, tragedy, pain, heartache, and extreme hardship made the stories golden. Those who lived told what happened from their point of view. Diaries of Mr. Breen and Virginia Reed documented daily what happened. Others felt the need to change what happened because they wished it hadn't happened or that they had acted differently.

Years Later

Virginia Reed would write in a letter after their return: *never take no cutoffs and hurry along as fast as you can.*

She did some journal writing and wrote about the trip. After arriving in Sutter's Fort in Sacramento, she decided not to marry the first man who proposed to her although there were many potential suitors. She went to school and after learning proper English and writing, she rewrote her journals saying she was embarrassed by the incorrect grammar and word usage. That was too bad because in comparison, some of the information she originally wrote had changed. She also wanted to become a Catholic because she deeply loved and respected Patrick Breen and his constant reading of the Bible to her. This did cause some consternation from her father, but he soon calmed down and welcomed her and her Catholic husband home. Virginia married John Murphy and they had nine children.

Patty Martha Reed married Frank Lewis and they had eight children.

Jimmy Reed, five years old when he was rescued, married Sarah Adams, while his brother Tommy never married. He also kept his promise that he would never be hungry again. He also claimed he would never walk again, but he did use both his legs for walking in the end.

James Reed moved his family to San Jose where he became quite active in civic duties. He and his wife Margaret, who no longer suffered from terrible headaches, had two more children. They were one of the two families who suffered no loss of family members during the long one-year migration to the west. James Reed was the only adult male to publish a book about the Donner Party.

Eliza, the cook for the Reeds, did find good fortune in California and she married within six months after her rescue.

Eliza Donner, who was only three at the time, grew up and married a widower Sherman O. Houghton. She was to write a book later about the Donner party after interviewing her sister about what happened.

George Donner, son of Jacob, was nine at the time of his rescue. He married Margaret Watson and they had eight children.

Both Donner families suffered great losses with so many dying. Tamsen, George, Jacob, Elizabeth, and sons, Samuel and Lewis, all died in the Alder Creek. Mary Donner, who was rescued twice–once after being abandoned in Starved Camp and having suffered frostbite and burning her foot when she fell in the fire. They thought she would die, but she healed and married Sherman O. Houghton. She died in 1860 and Sherman then married Mary's cousin, Eliza.

Remember Edward Breen? The lad who broke his leg riding his pony. He married twice. His first wife was Catherine and they had three children. Unfortunately, she died. He remarried Mary Jane Burns and had three more children.

Patrick Breen, not home more than a few months, got together with some others and made the trip back to the Donner Lake in June 1847 to see if they could salvage some goods. They were able to bring back some wagonloads of things that had not been pillaged. Patrick's diary, which he wrote in almost everyday, gives a good idea of what happened at the Donner Lake site and he gave an accounting of the weather on a daily basis. He then moved his family to San Juan Batista into a ranch on the San Andreas Fault.

Besides his son Edward, John Breen struck it rich in 1849. During the California Gold Rush, John brought home $12,000 worth of gold. He then married Leah Smith and they had ten children.

Mary Murphy married William Johnson, the man who owned the Johnson ranch which played a part in the refuge that the emigrants enjoyed after their rescue. He was an abusive man and in the beginning, she tolerated his treatment because she was an orphan and felt she had no choice. However, Mary divorced William and then married Charles Covillaud. Charles owned a large land plot with two other men. He then founded the town of Marysville, California, naming the town after his dear wife.

Mary Ann Graves married Edward Pyle within six months of her rescue with the Forlorn Hope. He died in a few years and she remarried J. T. Clarke. They had nine children.

Leanna, who was rescued in the First Relief, married John App and they had three children.

William Eddy, who lost his wife, young son, and daughter to the snowy hills of the Sierras remarried a widow, Mrs. P. Alfred, but they divorced after having two children. He then married once more to A. H. Pardee.

Lansford Hastings became a lawyer and never felt that he had to answer for his make believe writings of an unsubstantiated cut-off.

It is worth nothing that Isabella Breen, who was a one-year-old when she was rescued off the mountain, married Thomas McMahon and died in 1935. She was the last living direct survivor of the Donner Party.

Lewis Keseberg felt he was unjustly treated and made a slander suit and demanded $1000.00 against his accusers. He was awarded $1.00. There will always be suspicion about his role in the death of Tamsen Donner and maybe of someone else as well. He became a schooner captain and then ran the Lady Adams Hotel in San Francisco, which also housed a restaurant and this fueled the bad jokes for decades.

On June 6, 1918, Patty Reed Lewis, Eliza Donner Houghton, and Frances Donner Wilde joined the Nevada Governor in the dedication of the Donner Lake monument. The picture of the women with the Governor can be seen at the museum at the Donner Lake State Park. There is a large monument showing the heights of the snow fall for that year with the four standing in front of it. There is a wonderful museum with artifacts from the Donner/Reed party, and new items are added occasionally and they are building a larger museum. The interest in the Donner Party has not decreased in all these 160 plus years.

Author's note:

Although Lewis Keseberg is often regarded with contempt, there has been no documented evidence that Lewis Keseberg ever killed anyone. David Galloway has speculated it in his book. When Tamsen scratched at Keseberg's door, he thought she was a wolf and shot her, but there is no physical proof of this.

In 1996, the California Trail Days event which was held 150 years after the Donner Party tragedy included a play and a mock inquest to determine Lewis Keseberg's guilt or innocence in the death of Tamsen Donner. This was at the Peppermill Hotel-Casino in Reno. David Fennimore, English professor from University of Nevada, played the part of Keseberg.

This was the script that I wrote and performed.

I played the part of Margaret Reed. As Margaret, I was able to tell my story as I knew it. I felt Lewis Keseberg was very unfair and quite aggressive in the banishment of my husband, James Reed, in the death of John Snyder. The man, John Snyder, was cruel and unreasonable towards the oxen. My husband had objected and when John continued to whip the beasts, he tried to intercede. As I saw this, I became upset and rushed to his defense. John whipped me in the face. James became enraged, drew his knife, and stabbed John once. John died of that one knife stroke and James, my husband, was unfairly banished. It was Lewis Keseberg who raised the yoke of his wagon and offered to hang my husband immediately. He tried to rile up the crowd to kill James, but cooler heads prevailed.

I avoided Mr. Keseberg the rest of the trip although I was kind to his wife and baby and tried to help them and give her support.

I left the Donner Lake site and two of my babies had to turn back. That was my darkest hour, even darker than when my baby died before we set out on this fated trip. I felt the depths of despair when my Patty and Tommy had to turn back. I could have gone back with them or continued with Virginia and James. Virginia had almost died in the camp. I knew she would starve if we did not leave. I had to choose between my two sets of children. What a miserable day, what a miserable mother I thought I was.

Therefore, I can only guess what happened in the Donner Lake camp. Lewis Keseberg and Tamsen Donner were the last souls alive on March 30. On April 1, Tamsen was dead. God rest her soul. I cannot say what happened to that kind soul, my good friend. I only know the type of man Lewis Keseberg was when I left. I know adversity can change a man. I simply do not know.

At the 150th Donner Party California Day, it was interesting to meet descendants of the Donner party. Today, many of the descendants are leery of talking with writers or history buffs. Very often, people want to sensationalize what happened in the Sierras all those years ago. They are also very particular as to how their ancestors are portrayed and rightly so. Each one of us wants our families and ourselves to be remembered as upstanding, honest, and brave citizens. We owe the Donner party a debt of gratitude, and we owe the descendants a right to their privacy and the honor and respect their family names carry.

They are still excavating the sites of the Donner Lake and Alder Creek. As more items are found, they are revising some of the information. There have been some changes on where the cabins stood and how close they were to each other and to the Donner Lake, the Truckee River, and the Alder Creek. The types of cabins have been revised as well. It is now thought that the Donners eked out their existence in lean-tos with blankets and hides for walls. These would cover brush walls that they quickly threw together to survive the coming snowstorms. The cabins that the Breens, the Reeds, and the Graves lived in were quite short; meaning, the walls were maybe 4-5 feet tall and very dark. It is thought that the rooms stayed dark and were very smoky. With the terrible living conditions, the poor nutrition, the state of starvation, and the smoke these people inhaled, it is amazing that so many lived long lives and had children.

There is always question of whether there was actual cannibalism practiced. Practiced is the wrong word. These people were starving to death and they had a food source: human flesh. In order to live, they had to eat human flesh. A recent excavation found bones that revealed cuts made from knives that substantiate these claims. In addition, as you read the journals of the occupants of the Donner/ Reed party, they talk about what they had to do. As recounted in this story, a father tenderly tells his daughter she must eat his flesh. It is more important to live than to die and squander a food source. If any of us were in the same circumstance, I have no doubt that we would eat human flesh. Until one is faced with that desperate situation, no judgment can be made.

Bibliography

Burton, Gabrielle *Searching for Tamsen Donner*. University of Nebraska Press. 2009

DeVoto, Bernard *The Year of Decision 1846,* The Riverside Press, 1942

Hastings, Lansford W. *The Emigrants' Guide to Oregon and California,* 1845 Applewood reprint.

Houghton, Eliza P. Donner *The Expedition of the Donner Party and its Tragic Fate, Arthur H. Clark Co. 1911, Copyright 1996, reprinted 1998 Sierra District California State Parks.*

Johnson, Kristin *"Unfortunate Emigrants", Narratives of the Donner Party,* Utah State University Press. 1996

Keithley, George *The Donner Party,* George Broiler, Inc. 1972

Laugaard, Rachel K. *Patty Reed's Doll, The Story of the Donner Party.* McCurdy Historical Doll Museum, 1981

Lavender, David *Snowbound, The Tragic Story of the Donner Party* 1996

Limburg, Peter R. *Deceived, the story of the Donner Party.* IPSBooks 1998

Maino, Jeannette Gould. *Left Hand Turn, a Story of the Donner Party Women* 1987

McGlashan, C.F. *History of the Donner Party*, Stanford University Press 1940 revised 1947

McLaughlin, Mark *The Donner Party: Weathering the Storm,* MicMac Publishing

Mullen, Frank Jr. The Donner Party Chronicles, A day by day account of a doomed wagon train 1846-1847. A Halcyon Imprint of the Nevada Humanities Committee 1997

Murphy, Virginia Reed *Across the Plains In the Donner Party, A Personal Narrative of the Overland Trip to California* 1846-47. Vistabooks, 1995

Stewart, George R. *Ordeal By Hunger, The classic Story of the Donner Party.* Pocket Books, N.Y. 1936, 1960, 1971

Thornton, J. Quinn, *Camp Death: The Donner Party Mountain Camp 1846-47.* Outlooks, Inc. 1986

www.redravenbookdesign.com

Made in the USA
San Bernardino, CA
16 February 2017